Playing House

La Petite Mort Club Intimate Encounters

Ellis O. Day

I love to hear from readers so email me at
authorellisoday@gmail.com

Facebook
https://www.facebook.com/EllisODayRomanceAuthor/

Twitter
https://twitter.com/ellis_o_day

Pinterest
www.pinterest.com\AuthorEllisODay

Join My Readers' Group and for a limited time get the entire Six Nights of Sin series for FREE

(THERE'S A PEEK OF BOOK ONE AT THE END OF THIS STORY)

Click Here to Get Your FREE Books
Or go to my website
www.EllisODay.com

Here's What You Get When You
Join My Readers' Group

Win Before You Can Buy
Exclusive Giveaways
Free Books
Sneak Peeks

CHAPTER 1: SARAH

Sarah grabbed the takeout and grocery bags from her car and walked into the house. "Hey, boys. Can't pet you. Got my hands full here." She tried to push past her two dogs, but that was no easy feat. Tank was a Belgian Malinois, a retired military dog, and Sweetie was a pit-bull mix. One of them alone could block the doorway but both together, wiggling and wagging their tails could push her back into the garage.

"You need help?" hollered Nick from the living room.

"No. I got it." She squeezed between the two monsters and opened the laundry room door, stepping into the main part of the house.

Nick sat on the couch, glancing up from his laptop. "Wow. You got a lot of food. Want some help putting it away."

"No. Thanks." She headed into the kitchen. She was

the luckiest woman alive. Not only was he gorgeous—black hair, brown eyes and a body she drooled over—but he was the most helpful man she'd ever met, never skimping on doing more than his share of housework.

She dropped everything on the counter and began putting away the groceries. She slipped the dessert she'd gotten from her friend, Maggie, in the back of the refrigerator. She couldn't have him chowing down on it now. She may need that sugary safety net to assuage his temper after she told him she'd volunteered them to watch Maggie's three children this weekend.

Nick loved kids. He probably wouldn't mind babysitting but she should've asked him first. It'd been a spur of the moment thing and Maggie had been so excited. She couldn't back out now. She grabbed the takeout bags, opening the premade salad and dumping it into a bowl. "You ready to eat?"

"Always," he answered.

She jumped, her heart pounding. "You scared me."

"I see that." Nick stood in the doorway, looking sexy as always—hair a little too long and mussed, dark eyes roaming over her. His worn jeans hugged his body, letting her know that he was semi-aroused and making her heart race for an entirely different reason than surprise.

Would she ever quit turning into a quivering mess of desire when he looked at her? She hoped not, but she didn't have to let him know how he affected her. It was good for him to have to work for it. "I got salad and Thai food."

"Salad and Thai food? What kind of combination is

that?"

"Salad is good for us and Thai…that sounded good to me. Since you wouldn't tell me what you were hungry for when I called..." As soon as the words left her lips, she knew her mistake and her blood began to hum in anticipation.

"Oh, you know what I'm hungry for." He prowled closer. "What I'm always hungry for."

She moved to the other side of the table. They both knew how this would end but the game was always fun. "I meant to eat."

"Me too." His grin widened and his eyes darkened as they rested on the juncture between her thighs.

"For dinner. Eat for dinner." Suddenly, she wasn't so hungry.

"Dinner can wait." He stalked her.

"The food will get cold." She made sure to keep a table or a chair between them. The man was arrogance personified. She couldn't make her surrender too easy on him.

"Microwaves are a wonderful invention."

"Yes, they are but—"

"Stop running from me." He stepped closer and she moved away. "You know, I'll catch you."

"I don't know anything of the sort."

"I always win."

"There's a first time for everything." She had to admit she wasn't exactly a loser in these games.

"There is, but it won't be tonight."

"It might be." She kept circling the table, keeping pace with his steps.

"Let's bet." His wicked grin made her knees and everything else melt. "Anything and everything. I want you naked and doing my bidding all night."

"Ha." Hell, she'd do that anytime he asked, after she'd made him earn it. "That's not going to happen."

"I think it will. Bet me on who wins this game."

"I don't think so." She smiled as Tank wandered into the room. "I have reinforcements."

"Please. We worked out our differences a long time ago. He's on my side." Nick stopped at the counter and grabbed two dog cookies from the container.

"No fair. You're bribing him."

His hot gaze roamed over her, making her shiver. "I'll bribe you too if it'll work."

"It won't."

Tank trotted to the counter and Nick handed him a cookie.

This was her chance. She raced out of the kitchen.

"Shit."

She heard a cookie drop and then Nick was in the living room, only a few steps behind her. She headed for their bedroom.

"That's the right direction." He ran after her. "Don't you dare lock that door."

"Oh, I am so going to lock the door." She flew into the room, flinging the door shut but he slammed into it before she could lock it. She grabbed the handle, trying to keep him from opening it. To lock it, she'd have to let go with one hand and that wasn't going to work. She was barely keeping him out as it was. "Stop."

"*That* is not going to happen."

Her fingers clamped around the knob but it was no use. He was bigger and stronger than she was.

"You're cheating." She laughed as the door slid open a crack. She threw her weight against it but he pushed her backward anyway.

"How is this cheating?"

"You're bigger than me." Her feet scrambled on the floor, trying in vain to keep him out.

"I am that. And harder. Much, much harder. Painfully hard." He gave one more shove and then stepped into the room and pull her into his arms. "Hello." He kissed her.

His lips were soft and sweet, his hands roaming over her back and ass. She sighed as his mouth lifted from hers, her body boneless, wet and eager for him. "Hi."

"I missed you." He kissed her again, this one a little longer and deeper.

"I was only gone a few hours." She'd gone to therapy today and then the store.

"Don't care. I missed you." His lips trailed down her throat and she tipped her head, giving him better access.

The man had the mouth of a magician. Everywhere he kissed lit a fire. It didn't matter where his lips touched—her nose, her knuckles—all paths linked to her pussy.

"And just so you know." He cupped her ass. "I win."

"You cheated."

"How? How did I cheat?" He lifted her and strode across the room.

"You used your strength."

"That's not cheating." He tossed her on the bed and pulled off his shirt.

"Is too." This game wasn't done yet. She rolled over and scrambled across the bed, dropping to the floor.

He smirked at her, his broad muscular chest now bare and making her mouth water. She couldn't wait to run her hands all over all that smooth, hot skin.

"Nice try, but you're not getting away." He pulled off his belt.

She forced her eyes away from him and took a small step toward the bathroom.

"I don't think so." He stepped to the side, blocking that path.

It was exactly what she'd wanted him to do. She grabbed a pillow, flung it at him and ran for the bedroom door.

"Hey!"

In a second, she was in the living room and heading for the garage, Nick right behind her.

"Now, who's the cheater?" His arm snaked around her waist, pulling her back flush against his front. "I see you're going to make me work for it tonight." His lips trailed kisses down her neck as his hands cupped her breasts.

"Of course." She tipped her head and arched her back, pressing into his touch.

His hands drifted to the bottom of her shirt teasing

along the skin above her pants. He grabbed the shirt and lifted. She raised her arms and he pulled it off, tossing it on the floor. He unhooked her bra, kissing along her back and then down. She let the bra hang loose as he knelt behind her cupping her ass.

He kissed the small of her back, grinning against her skin. "Wait right there." He stood.

"Where are you going?" Now that he'd caught her, she was eager to get on with the fucking.

"You'll see." He took another step toward the kitchen and stopped. "I don't trust you."

"What?" She really hadn't thought about running again, jumping him maybe but escaping? Nope. "Me?"

"Yeah. You." He grabbed her hand—"you're coming with me"—and dragged her into the kitchen. He spun a chair away from the table.

"What do you want with that?" Images of her straddling him or leaning over it while he fucked her from behind filled her head and made her pussy melt. They'd both be fun and she couldn't wait to do one of them and then later the other.

"You'll see." He picked up the chair and nudged her with his shoulder, keeping her hand in his. "Go. Back to the living room."

"Yes, Sir."

"That's a game for another time." His voice was thick with desire.

"Yes, it is. So is professor." She grinned at him.

He groaned. "We need to do that again. It's been a

while since the dirty professor has gotten any action."

"Yes, it has." She did miss her professor.

He put the chair down and then sat. "Now, come here I want to see your bra and panties."

She frowned at him, having no idea where he was going with this. "You can't exactly miss the bra." The only thing keeping it up was her hand.

"And I saw it the other night at the Viewing, but I want to see it up close."

Ah, that was the game. Her legs quivered. This was going to end a lot differently than that first meeting. "No touching."

"Okay." The sparkle in his eyes told her she was missing something.

She moved closer, facing him and holding the loose bra against her chest.

"Move your hands."

"It's too loose."

"Not my problem."

"Ah. There's the dick from that day. I knew he was around here somewhere." He'd been a jerk but such a hot and sexy one that she'd still agreed to spend six nights with him. She was so glad she had. She'd planned on a few evenings of great sex and instead had found the love of her life.

"And here's the dick you're going to get to know very well." He grabbed one of her hands, placing it on his cock.

She burst out laughing.

"Hey, that does not help a man's ego." He dropped his

hold on her hand.

"Oh, please." She cupped her bra to her breasts. "Your ego is made of armor; it never even dents."

"When you're good, you're good."

She rolled her eyes, but he was very good and they both knew it.

"Now, move your hands."

"Okay." She reached behind her to re-hook her bra.

"Stop. No refastening of clothes."

"Who says?"

"I do and…" He grabbed a paper from the coffee table. "It's in our contract."

"Is it?" That paper was a flyer for a credit card.

"It is. You agreed." He tried not to smirk. "To everything I said."

She snorted. "Did I?"

"Yep." He lost his battle and one part of his mouth tipped upward.

"Doesn't sound like me."

"Don't know about that. We just met, but you did agree." His dark eyes danced with humor.

"Hmm. I don't remember that. I think I need to read it to see what I agreed to."

"You can read it later. Trust me on this one."

She raised her brow and he shrugged.

"Okay." Her brain wanted to argue, but her nipples were hard and her body wanted his hands on her. Sometimes, she had to let her body win. She dropped her hands to her sides. The bra stayed in place but gaped around her breasts.

"Come closer." The humor in his eyes had been replaced by lust.

She moved forward, not even thinking about disobeying his command.

"Closer."

"No touching, remember?" She had to stay in the game. They'd just met. She hadn't even agreed to sleep with him, but her body wasn't playing. It knew what pleasure those hands and lips could bring.

"I remember." He crooked his finger and she stepped closer, stopping right in front of his legs.

"Bend down." His eyes were locked on her chest.

"You can see the bra from here."

"Not the inside."

"The inside?" That was new.

"I want to see the stitching. Make sure it's well made." His eyes lifted to hers. They were dark and hot. "I don't want anything marring that perfect skin if I'm going to be in charge of it for six weeks."

"In charge. I know I didn't agree to that." She liked to be in control—to tease him and make him beg—and she also liked it when he was in charge.

"But you did. You agreed to be in charge of my body and I'm in charge of yours."

"Oh. That could work." *Deliciously well*. She shivered as she leaned forward, letting the bra gape, her pussy humming at the heated gleam in his eyes.

"May I?" His eyes met hers as he held out his hand. "I

won't touch you."

"Yes." She couldn't deny him anything.

He hooked his finger in the cloth between her breasts and pulled downward. She inhaled deeply, causing his finger to brush gently across her skin.

His eyes darkened as he removed the bra, letting it fall to the floor. Her nipples puckered in anticipation as his gaze burned, hot and heavy on her breasts. He moved closer, his lips a fraction away from her painful peaks. Peaks that needed the soothing of his tongue and mouth.

"Beautiful." His hot breath teased over her skin and then he straightened. "Now, your underwear."

It took everything she had not to grab his head and pull him to her chest but their games were better the longer they played. "Okay, but remember, no touching."

He forced his eyes upward, a slight smirk on his handsome lips. "How could I forget?"

She nodded and unbuttoned her jeans. She swore she could feel the heat from his gaze as his eyes locked onto her fingers. His nostrils flared as she unzipped her pants, sliding them slowly down before stopping when they were right above her pussy.

"Keep going." His voice was a rough whisper, his breath hot against her abdomen.

"No. You can see my underwear."

He looked up at her, the muscle in his cheek throbbing. He was growing tired of the game and that made it so much more fun. She loved teasing him until he lost control.

"I can only see part. I want to see all of them. How

they fit your ass and"—his eyes gleamed—"how they cradle your pussy."

Her breath hitched and she cleared her throat, pushing down her desire. "That's a problem."

"Why?" His brow raised.

"I still have my shoes on." It was time to test his limits.

His eyes dropped to her feet and back to her face, a hint of confusion in his gaze. "Then take them off."

"I would but I have to"—she bit her lower lip, making sure he could see her teeth and her tongue dart out to lick away the sting—"ask you a favor."

"Of course, what is it?" His gaze sharpened, sensing the trap, but he played along.

"Do you mind if I touch you? Only to support myself while I take off my shoes."

"Not at all." His wicked grin sent a flood of moisture between her legs.

"Remember. No touching." This was probably going to put an end to their game, but that was okay. They could always play later.

"Doesn't seem fair, but okay." He sent her a playful glare.

She touched his shoulder, leaning forward and putting her breasts right in front of his face as she lifted her leg. The muscles under her hand tightened but he didn't move. Drat the man. "Now, the other one." She shifted, gasping slightly as her breast grazed his cheek, his five o'clock shadow scraping against her nipple. "All done." She hesitated for a moment, waiting for him to lose control, to grab her or at least kiss her breast.

"Glad to be of assistance." He leaned back in the chair, pulling away from her hand and smirking up at her. "Now, let me see those underwear."

She glared at him as she slid her pants down.

"Nice, very nice." His hot, dark gaze followed her hands.

Nice, her ass. She kicked the pants out of the way, leaving her legs spread slightly. The light green of her panties was darker in the crotch from her wetness.

His smirk disappeared as his face tightened with lust. He cleared his throat. "Did you spill something?"

"What?" She feigned shock. "Where?"

He nodded. His eyes glued to her pussy.

"Hmm. You're right. They are wet." She put her hand between her legs, running her finger over the satin of her panties and sighing.

"Yes, they are." His voice was raspy with need.

"Not sure what caused that." She raised her hand to her mouth but he still stared at her pussy. "Maybe I should taste it and see."

His eyes shot to her face.

She slowly slipped her finger between her lips. "Mmm. Not sure what this is."

He groaned. It was desperate and needy. "I know."

"How would you know what I spilled on my panties?"

"Trust me, I know."

"Maybe you should taste to be sure."

"That's an excellent idea." He reached for her but she

stepped back.

"From my finger."

His eyes narrowed as he watched the slow descent of her hand—down her chest, between her breasts, over her abdomen and finally between her legs.

"It'd be better if you went beneath the underwear."

"You think?" Her finger slid back and forth, rubbing her panties along her pussy. Her breath hitched as she increased the pressure. If he didn't get moving, she'd come while he watched.

"I do. Take off your underwear."

"Oh, I don't have to do that." Her hand slid into her panties. "I can—"

"Take them off." He snapped, his control frazzling.

"If you think that's best." She pulled her hand from her underwear and rubbed circles along her clit.

"I do. Now." His arms shook as his hands clenched the sides of the chair.

She shimmied them down her hips, making sure to add an extra wiggle for his viewing pleasure. She kicked them aside and skimmed her hand up her inner thigh and to her pussy. She was slick with need and desire as her finger played between her folds.

"Enough."

Her hand stilled.

"I get to taste."

"I wanted to make sure I had enough for you to identify it."

"It's plenty." He grabbed her wrist and opened his

mouth, licking and sucking the juices from her finger. Her pussy clenched wanting that tongue and mouth on it. He pulled her hand away from his face, frowning.

"What's wrong?" Now, she sensed a trap.

"Not sure. I need another taste."

"Okay, by me." She started to move her hand but he tightened his grip.

"I think your finger altered the flavor." His eyes gleamed wickedly. "I should taste it directly from the source."

"Really?" Her body trembled in anticipation, knowing exactly where this was leading.

"Yes.

"But you're not allowed to touch me."

"Hold yourself open and I'll use my tongue."

"That's still touching."

"No, it isn't. Touching is with hands." He waved at her.

"No." So, that'd been his plan all along. "You can touch someone with your tongue or foot or—"

"Breasts." He tapped his cheek.

"I wasn't told I couldn't touch."

"Okay." He tipped his head, conceding the point. "But I disagree that touching with the tongue is actually touching. When people kiss, French kiss, they don't call it touching. Right?"

"No, but—"

"And when you eat an ice cream cone, you lick it, not touch it."

"Yes, but I don't use the word *touch* to describe holding a cone with my hands either." Her brain screeched to a halt as his look of triumph.

"Good point. I guess using my hands isn't touching either then."

"That's not what I meant."

"That's what I heard." He shrugged.

"Come on. You can't argue that you don't touch with your hands."

"Watch me. I can argue any point."

"I believe that." Some of her favorite moments of foreplay were their verbal bantering.

"But I'll give you the hands but not the tongue."

"Really?"

He laughed. "That did not come out right because I plan on giving you both." His gaze raked over her body.

She squeezed her legs together, trying to ease some of the ache so they could keep playing.

His handsome lips curved upward in a smirk. "I think you need to let me show you what I mean and then you decide if I'm touching you or not."

"Hmm." Right now, she was so horny she was going to jump him.

"I promise, if you think my tongue is the same as my hand or finger, you can stop me."

She took a deep breath, forcing her mind back to the game and not the pleasure that was coming her way. "I'm not sure about this."

"Trust me."

She laughed. "Oh, now I know I'm in trouble."

"You will be if you don't..."

She pulled the folds of her pussy open for him. "Just a little taste. Only enough so I can decide if touching with your tongue is the same as touching with your finger."

He inhaled deeply as he lowered his face, his hot breath wafting over her and making her shiver. The tip of his tongue slid gently over her folds before circling her clit. Her legs trembled and her belly clenched.

"I think, I should use my lips too." His hot breath teased her sensitive flesh.

"Yes." She tangled one hand in his thick, dark hair as he licked, up and down, slow and steady. He probed at her opening and then his mouth covered her clit, sucking. Her fingers dug into his scalp as her hips bucked against his face. She was so close. All she needed was a little more and she'd come.

He grabbed her ass and pulled her closer as he dropped to his knees, devouring her. All she could do was hang on as his tongue teased her clit and his fingers slid inside her stroking.

"Oh...Nick..."

He lifted her leg, placing it on the chair behind him and opening her wider. His one hand cradled her ass, his strength the only thing keeping her upright as he curled his fingers, finding her g-spot at the same time he suckled her clit. She moaned as pleasure shot through her, making her hips buck against his face as she broke apart.

CHAPTER 2: NICK

Nick couldn't wait a minute longer to get inside Sarah. He slid his fingers from her body and lifted her off her feet, carefully placing her on the floor. His dick hardened even more as she trembled from her orgasm. He was going to push her right into another one. He undid his pants, shoving them and his underwear out of his way.

She stared up at him, her green eyes half-closed and heavy as she spread her legs, welcoming him. He groaned. She was pink, wet perfection and she was his. He leaned over her, surrounding her with his large body as he guided his cock to her opening.

He'd never imagined sex could feel this good. He'd always loved to fuck but this was…more. Inside Sarah he felt at home, right, perfect. She inhaled as he pushed all the way in with one hard thrust. His heart thudded and his balls tightened but now that he was where he belonged, he was in no hurry. He brushed the hair from her face. She was so beautiful, red hair soft and long, vibrant green eyes. She was his fairy and he was never letting her go.

"I don't think that's your tongue." She smiled up at him.

"No?" He rocked into her slow and deep. "You sure?"

"Yeah." She sighed. "I'm pretty sure." She relaxed into his pace, moving with him.

"Hmm." He leaned down to kiss her; he had to. She was just too cute as she tried to keep their game alive.

His desire, banked only a moment ago, revved back to life as she opened for him, her tongue tangling with his. The games were done. His thrusts came harder and faster. He cupped her cheeks, holding her while his tongue plunged into her mouth like his dick ravaged her body.

Her breath came in pants and she tangled one of her hands in his hair as the other one caressed his back. Her legs wrapped around his hips, pulling him closer. His body screamed for him to pump harder, faster, race to that glorious finish but he wasn't ready to be done fucking her yet.

"Hey, let's slow down." He lifted off her a second, slowing his thrusts and moaning as her legs and pussy tightened around him.

"Why?"

He grinned. She liked to come hard and fast. "Because you feel so fucking good." He could stay buried inside her forever, her body pulsing around his, squeezing him, loving him.

"You do too." She tightened her inner muscles.

"Stop that." He groaned, his hips picking up their pace.

"What? This?' She did it again.

"Yes. Fuck. You win." He couldn't deny her or himself any longer. He lowered his body back to hers, holding himself up with his arms as he shoved into her, his thrusts hard and fast. She gasped, her nails digging into his back, spurring him on. There was nothing but pleasure. No room. No house. Nothing but his body and hers coming together. Her long, silky limbs tangled with his as the sound of moans and flesh slapping against flesh filled his head.

She clamped around him, hot and tight. Perfect. He wasn't going to last much longer and neither was she. Her hips bucked against him, her eyes closed, her face tight as she searched for her pleasure. He slid his hand between them, teasing her clit. She gasped and he pumped into her hard and deep as his finger circled her tiny bud faster and faster.

"Ohhh…." Her body convulsed around his, squeezing his cock.

It was too much. Pleasure shot from his dick through his spine and to his balls. "Sarah…" He groaned as he came, collapsing on top of her. He kissed her neck, unwilling to move. He should. They were on the floor. She couldn't be comfortable but he'd worked too hard to get here to leave now. He rolled to his side, pulling her with him and keeping his dick still partially inside her.

"I'm hungry." She kissed his chest.

"Give me a few minutes and I'll be ready—"

"For food." She slapped him playfully. "Don't you ever get enough?"

"Of you? Never." He ran his hand through her hair.

Her eyes softened and she kissed him. "I love you."

"I love you too."

"But I'm starving." She lifted her leg to get up.

"Wait." He grabbed her thigh, stopping her. "I want to stay inside you a little longer."

"Oh no." She kissed him again, nipping his bottom lip. "I know you too well. A little longer will turn into another round and then I won't eat for hours." She moved his hand off her leg. "Now, let me go so I can eat."

"I don't want to." He sounded like a kid but he didn't care. He'd waited all day for this.

"But, I'm hungry. I promise, after we eat, we can lie in bed and snuggle."

"I don't snuggle." He snorted.

"Then, what do you call this?"

"Having a hot, gorgeous woman draped over my body, keeping my dick warm is not snuggling."

"Oh, is that what I am? Your dick warmer?"

"You are my dick's everything."

"Please." She rolled her eyes and shifted off him.

He sat, pulling up his pants. "You are. You make it happy. You make it sad."

"How do I make it sad?" She pulled on her underwear.

"When you leave it." He looked down at his flaccid penis. "See how sad it looks."

"It does that."

He laughed and zipped up. "You even kiss it to make it feel better." He stood, grabbing a shirt from the laundry basket he'd left on the chair and sliding it over his head. "And since you were the one who made it sad..." He raised his eyebrow.

"You're saying I owe you a blow job." She grabbed one of his shirts from the basket and slipped it on as she headed for the kitchen.

"Owe is a strong word."

"Good answer." She laughed.

He grabbed her around the waist. "You sit. I'll make dinner."

"You'll make dinner?" she asked incredulously.

"Yep."

"You mean the takeout?"

He tightened his arms around her, shuffling her to a chair. "Yes." He walked to the fridge and poured a glass of wine, taking it to her. "You relax and I'll get everything ready."

"Hmm. Working for that blow job, are we?"

"You know me so well."

"It's not your worst plan."

"You know what?" He grinned as her eyes roamed over his body. "It's hot in here. " He pulled off his shirt.

"Nice move." Her eyes brightened as she sipped her wine and stared at his chest.

He swore he could feel the heat from her gaze. She was as horny for him as he was for her and that made their relationship perfect. He bent and kissed her. "Better turn it down a notch or we won't be eating...food anytime soon."

"Oh, no. I am eating that Thai food even if I have to tie

you up."

"That can be arranged." He preferred to be in charge but Sarah did like to run their sexcapades every now and then.

"Go." She swatted his ass. "Feed me."

"Okay, but you owe me." He walked to the counter and put one of the containers in the microwave.

"Owe you? For letting me eat?"

"Yep." He poured the other takeout container into a bowl. When the microwave beeped, he switched them.

"That doesn't seem right, especially since I brought the food home. All you're doing is dumping it into dishes and heating it up."

He shrugged. "Can't help it. That's how the world works." He emptied the warm food into a dish and carried it, silverware and two plates to the table. "Plus, I am waiting on you."

"Fine. I owe you." She poured some of the Pad Thai on her plate.

"Excellent." He grabbed the other dish from the microwave and a water from the refrigerator.

"But you owe me for bringing the food home."

"That seems fair." He sat, putting half of the Red Curry on his plate.

She took a bite and sighed. "This is so good."

His gaze went to her lips as she ate. She was exquisite and all his. He had no idea how he'd gotten so lucky to get her but he wasn't going to lose her—ever. They couldn't get married soon enough for him, but she didn't seem to be in any hurry. He ate more, glancing at her. Lately, he'd been avoiding all talk of their wedding because it always ended with a fight but he was tired of waiting. "So, how about a spring wedding?"

She chewed and swallowed taking a sip of her wine. "We'd have to have both indoor and outdoor facilities in case the weather is bad."

"Sure." He didn't care about any of that. He just wanted her to be his.

"Hmm." She took another bite of her dinner. "If it's rainy that could get messy."

"I like messy." He let his eyes drop to her mouth. "The messier the better." His gazed lowered to her breasts. He loved seeing his sperm on her body, slick and wet, marking her as his.

"For sex, yes, but not for our wedding."

"If you say so." He took a gulp of his water. "Then how about summer. That'll give you a few months."

She choked on her food, taking a quick drink. "You were talking about this spring?"

"Yeah." He frowned. "What spring did you think I meant?"

"Next year or the year after."

"No." He put his fork down. "I'm not waiting that long."

"Weddings take time to plan."

"You've had months." He was tired of her delays.

"I told you, I wasn't doing anything about our wedding until I was sure we were getting married." Her cheeks flushed with temper.

"There was no if. You agreed." He didn't care if she got pissed. He was done with this shit.

"And then I found out you didn't want a prenup and I took back my yes until you smartened up."

"Until I…" His jaw clenched and he took a deep breath. "Prenup is signed. Now, we get married."

"Exactly. In a year or—"

"No. Two months."

"I can't plan a weeding in two months. Not the giant event you want."

"I don't want a big wedding."

"Yes, you do."

"No. I do not. I want my family and some friends."

"Your family is huge and you don't only want the immediate family. You want cousins and second cousins."

"They're family. I have to invite them."

Her eyes softened. "I know, but I need time to plan that."

"I'll help." His dick perked to life at the idea.

"We tried that and it didn't work."

He couldn't hold back a grin. "I thought it worked great." Every time they started planning the wedding, they'd ended up fucking like rabbits.

"I'm not kidding, Nick. I need time." She touched his hand. "Why don't we set a date…or month and then I can—"

"Plan?" He pulled his hand away. "You've had more than enough time. You should've thought about all this when you decided to be stubborn about the damn prenup." He picked up his dish and carried it to the counter. "Don't blame me because you didn't utilize your time wisely."

She dropped her fork. "Then, I guess you'll be marrying yourself in two months because I won't be there."

"Oh, you'll be there even if I have to throw you over my shoulder and carry you down the aisle."

"That is not going to happen." She stood, taking her dish to the counter.

"Sarah. I want to marry you." He walked up behind her, running his hands down her arms, trying to smooth away her anger. "Why are you putting this off?"

"I'm not."

"You are and you shouldn't. You love me."

"You are so cocky." She didn't laugh but she softened under his hands.

"It's not cocky if it's true."

She shook her head and turned in his arms. "I want to marry you." She touched his cheek, smiling softly at him. "We could elope."

"My family would kill me. Your family would kill me." He grabbed her hips, pulling her closer.

"Then we need to do it right and that takes time."

"Take a lesson from Terry's book. Throw money at it." That was his friend's answer to every problem.

"It didn't work with Maggie and it won't work for our wedding. The good venues are booked for months, sometimes years. Paying extra won't help."

"Okay." He didn't like it but he wanted her to have the

wedding of her dreams. He rested his forehead on hers. "Hurry. Please."

"I'll talk to Maise. My sister is great with this stuff."

"And Annie. Get Annie on it. She'll badger everyone and get it done in no time."

"Patrick might not be happy with us for tying up his girlfriend's free time."

"Screw Patrick. I want you as my wife." He kissed her, his hands skimming under her shirt and across her stomach. His thumb caressed her flat belly. "I want my kid inside you. I want a family with you." He kissed her again. "And you can help Annie when she and Patrick get married."

"I will, of course, but you don't get to volunteer me for it." She poked his stomach.

"Sorry, but that's part of being a couple."

"Is that so?"

"Yep. Heard every couple I know complain about it."

"I'm glad you feel that way."

"Why?" His hand stilled. From the gleam in her eyes he was in for a surprise and not an enjoyable one.

"We're watching Maggie's kids this weekend." She stepped to the side and walked to the table.

"We're what?" He liked kids. He wanted kids—a house full of them like how he'd grown up—but he didn't want to babysit three kids he barely knew.

"Maggie is taking Terry to the Club for his birthday." She grabbed her wine glass.

"I thought they were having their bedroom soundproofed." Which was an excellent idea that he was going to copy. That way nothing, not even kids, would disrupt their alone time. They could be as loud and kinky as they wanted while their kids slept peacefully in another room.

"They are. They'll be gone for a week—"

"We're watching her kids for a week?" He hadn't meant his words to come out as loudly as they had but a week!

"No." She finished her wine and grabbed the bottle from the refrigerator, refilling her glass. "Just Friday night through Sunday afternoon."

"Oh." That was better but still not good. "Why are we doing this?"

"Her ex was going to keep them but he cancelled at the last minute."

"I thought her kids were going with them."

"To the Club?" She frowned at him.

"They're going to the Club?"

"I told you." She sighed in exasperation. "She's taking Terry to the Club this weekend." Her eyes sparkled. "It'll be Maggie's first time there as a couple."

"And as a Sub." He grabbed a beer from the fridge. "They can't take her kids to the Club but that's what babysitters are for. Can't she get one of those?"

"She did. Us."

"Oh. Isn't there someone else?"

"Like who? Annie and Patrick are at a funeral. She can't leave them with strangers for an entire weekend. She has no family and Terry's kids aren't in the area."

"So, you volunteered us." There was more to this. He could see it in her sharp, green eyes.

"Yes. She's my friend and she's been planning this for a long time. I didn't want her to cancel because her ex changed his mind." She took a sip of her wine. "People do that you know. Babysitters cancel. Plans fall through. You have to be flexible when you have kids."

"You think this weekend is going to change my mind about wanting kids."

"Not about wanting kids. I want kids too, just not yet. We're not even married."

"And whose fault is that?"

"Yours for taking forever to agree to the prenup."

He swore his teeth lost an inch from grinding. "No. It's yours for being so fucking stubborn."

"I think the word you're looking for is smart." She crossed her arms over her chest, making the shirt rise a bit and displaying more of her long, shapely legs.

His mouth watered but he forced his eyes to hers. "This weekend…whatever you think you're going to teach me, you won't." He took a step toward her. "I want kids. I want kids with you and I want them as soon as possible." He smirked. "I'd tamper with your birth control if I didn't think you'd kill me."

"That's a douche move."

"I know but I like to win."

"I'd leave you." The humor had fled from her face.

"Sarah." He took her hands in his. "I was kidding." He waited but she only stared at him. This was insulting. "You know I wouldn't do that."

"I know you like to win at any cost."

"Not that one." He kissed her softly. "I'd never hurt you like that." He wished she'd trust him but the doctor had said it'd take time. It might make him crazy but he'd force himself to give her as much as she needed.

"I know." She leaned against him. "I'm sorry I'm like this."

"No." He kissed her. "I shouldn't have said that. It was stupid."

"You were joking. It wasn't funny but I should trust you...I do trust you...I...sometimes..."

"I know." His arms tightened around her. He'd do anything to make her feel safe and loved but he couldn't force her. He hated it but he had to give her the time to get there on her own.

She leaned back. "Perhaps, we should bet on this weekend. Since you like to win. Let's wager."

When topics became too real, too close to her pain, she challenged him or seduced him to change the subject. He almost called her on it but the hint of pleading in her eyes froze his words. Dr. Smileworth had told him numerous times that pushing Sarah would make things worse, so he forced himself to play along. "What kind of bet?"

"I bet after spending an entire weekend with three kids, you'll change your mind about wanting your own right now."

"I won't." He'd been around his nieces and nephews enough to know that kids were great.

"I think you will."

"What do I win when I prove you wrong?"

"Whatever you want?"

"Don't say that if you don't mean it."

She smiled. "I do mean it." She ran her hand up his chest. "You can have whatever you want. Nothing is off the table."

"Come." There was no way was he letting that offer pass. He grabbed her hand and pulled her into the living room and over to his desk. He took a paper from the printer and wrote down her offer. "Sign."

CHAPTER 3: SARAH

"You're kidding?" Sarah stared at the pen in Nick's hand.

"Nope. I want this in writing."

"Why?" She studied him. The gleam in his dark eyes made her nervous.

"Because when I win, I don't trust you not to try and weasel out of this bet."

"Hey. I'd never do that. I'm a woman of my word."

He leaned closer, his lips brushing against her ear. "But you don't know what I'm going to ask you to do."

His breath on her neck sent those delicious heat filled words straight to her pussy. "I can't think of anything that I wouldn't be willing to do." It was true. She'd try anything he wanted. She thought she already had.

"Then you have no reason not to sign."

She still didn't trust him but she took the pen. "Is it anal?" That had been the one thing she'd refused to try. It didn't appeal to her although after talking to Annie she was curious.

"You'll have to wait until I win to find out." He tapped the paper, raising his brow in challenge.

"What do I get if I win?" She scribbled her name across the bottom.

"What do you want?" His voice was dark with promise.

"Hmm." She tamped down her desire. "How about you make the same wager?"

"Sure." He jotted it down on the paper and paused. "Are you sure? I already let you have anything you want that I can give you."

Her heart melted. Lord she loved this man and it terrified her. It could all be gone in a flash—an accident, an argument.

"But what are you supposed to learn from this?" He smirked at her. "Besides don't bet me because I always win."

"Me?"

"Yes. You think I'll learn how difficult it is having kids around and I think I'll love it. Not every minute but overall. So, what are you going to learn for your part of the bet?"

"Uhm…"

"I think"—he stepped closer to her—"that you'll learn how great I am with kids and that having me as the father of your children will be better than good."

"Oh Nick, that's not…I know you'll be a good father." She hated that her fears made him think she doubted him.

"You say it, but I don't think you truly believe it." He

placed his hand over her heart. "In here you want to believe it, but in here"—he kissed her forehead—"you're scared."

Her heart raced. He was getting too close to the truth. She was terrified but not of him as a father. She'd been pregnant once and had miscarried. What if she couldn't carry to term? He wanted kids so badly.

"Sarah?" He studied her a long moment, seeming to see into her mind. "What's wrong?"

Love was fragile. It could be destroyed by the tiniest thing. His family was huge and he wanted that kind of life. If she couldn't have children where would that leave them? Panic started to coil in her stomach, crawling its way up her throat. The room began to spin. She took a deep breath. She hadn't had an attack in over a year. She couldn't have one now. "Are you going to sign the paper or are you scared of what I'll ask you to do when I win." Her hand skimmed down his chest to the button of his pants.

"Are you okay?" He grabbed her wrist.

"Perfect." *No, but she would be.* He could take her away from her fears. Make her forget everything but him and her. "But I think it's time to pay you back." She let her tongue dart out and wet her lower lip a little as her hand pressed on his abdomen. "Sign the paper."

His grip loosened and she ran her hand down the bulge in his jeans. The coil of panic dissipated, replace by lust. She squeezed him through his pants as he scrawled his name on the paper.

"You know." She unbuttoned his pants. "We won't be able to be so spontaneous with a houseful of kids." She

34

slowly pulled down the zipper, watching as his chest began to heave.

"We'll figure something out." He leaned against the desk, spreading his legs.

"Hmm." She got down on her knees and shifted forward, kissing him through his underwear.

His hand came to her head, stroking her hair and coaxing her toward his groin.

"Hold onto the table." She loved being in charge, making this strong, alpha male bow to her demands. His eyes darkened but he did as she said. She knew it wouldn't last long. "I think that's what I'll ask for when I win."

"To give me blow jobs?" He smiled, disobeying her already and skimming his thumb over her lips. "In case this wasn't clear, you can suck my dick anytime you want."

She pulled his thumb into his mouth, teasing his pad with her tongue before nipping him and making him groan. "No, not giving you head." She grabbed his jeans and yanked them down. "What I want."

He stepped out of his pants.

She slid her finger inside the opening in his underwear, running it up and down his smooth, hot sex. She rested her cheek against him, inhaling the musky scent of his arousal.

"What do you want?" His hand tangled in her hair. "Right now, I'll agree to anything to get you to wrap those lips around my dick."

"What I want"—she leaned away, taking his hand from her head—"is to be in charge."

"You're going to have my dick in your mouth. You'll

be in charge."

"No, you'll cheat." She pulled down his underwear, his cock long and hard bobbing in front of her face.

"I don't cheat."

"You do. You say you'll let me be in charge and then you take over."

"I do not."

"You do." She stroked his dick, breathing on him but not touching him with her lips or tongue. "Even when I handcuff you, you find—"

"It's not my fault I know where the safety latch is." His eyes were like hot coals, dark and gleaming. "Please, I'm dying here."

"It's your fault you unhook yourself. You could try to have some self-control."

"I do try." His words came out between his gritted teeth. "I'm trying now."

"Not hard enough." She ran the velvety soft tip of his dick over her lips.

"You can see, it's plenty hard."

She touched him with the tip of her tongue. "When I win and I will because even though you'll be a great dad, you don't understand how much kids get in the way of"— she licked around the tip of his dick—"adult time, I'm going to be in charge. Completely in charge."

CHAPTER 4: NICK

"You won't win." Nick grasped the table so hard he was pretty sure there'd be indentations in the wood.

"I will." Sarah's tongue teased along his length.

He was going to explode or collapse, sobbing with frustration if she didn't take him in her mouth soon. "Enough, Sarah. Please." His hips thrust forward, his dick rubbing along her face.

"What's the matter, Nick? Don't like to be teased?"

"You've teased enough." His arms shook as he fought not to grab her head and urge her to get on with it.

"That's how I feel when you tease me, but you're bigger and stronger. You're in charge."

Her hot breath whispered across his aching cock but it wasn't enough. He needed her mouth. "You haven't won yet." He grabbed her head, tipping up her face. "Open."

"Let go of me." Her green eyes sparkled with challenge.

"You'll pay for this." He dropped his hands, his eyes locked on her mouth as if he could force it open with his will.

She ran her tongue over her lush pink lips and then opened. He groaned, grabbing his dick and placing it right in front of her face. It took everything he had not to grab her head and push inside that wet, hot heaven.

She leaned back. "Let go of your dick, or I stop."

"Fuck." He grabbed the table again.

"Don't worry. You'll get a reward for obeying."

"Please." *Fuck him.* She was making him beg but right now, he didn't care. Later, he'd get his revenge.

Her tongue came out, slowly licking up his staff and his legs shook.

"If you move your hands from the table, I stop. Understand?"

"Yes." His eyes locked with hers.

"Good boy."

"I'm not a fucking dog."

"You're panting like one."

A burst of laughter broke from his chest. "You are in so much trouble. I'm going…"

Her lips wrapped around his dick and all thought left his head as pleasure shot through his body. A guttural moan escaped his lips as she took him deeper. She was learning to deep throat but she didn't do it every time.

"Fuck." He hissed as her throat squeezed his dick. He tried not to thrust, tried to let her set the pace but his hips had a mind of their own.

She gagged and pulled off him, using her hands to spread her saliva on his cock.

"Sorry." He touched her cheek. Her eyes were watery but she smiled up at him and he fell in love with her even more. She was so fucking hot and kind and caring and everything he wanted. "Come here." He grabbed her arm.

"I'm not done yet." She pushed his hand away.

"I want to bury myself inside you. Feel you come on my cock." He grabbed her again.

She slapped his hand. "And I want to suck you until you can't take anymore."

"Deep throat me again and you'll be there."

"Fantastic." She slid his dick into her mouth.

As much as he wanted to watch her suck him off, his eyes drifted closed from the pleasure of her mouth. She was so tight, her tongue rubbing at his cock while he slid farther into her throat. His balls tightened and his spine tingled. "Fuck. I'm gonna come." His fingers tangled in her hair, not sure if he was going to push her away or pull her closer. She took that decision from him as she sucked harder and cupped his balls, squeezing gently. It was too much. He couldn't hold back anymore. He groaned, his hips thrusting into her mouth as he came.

She pulled off him, gagging a bit. His sperm slipped from her lips. She was his. Marked. Branded by him. He ran his hand over her chin, capturing his seed. She opened her mouth but he trailed his fingers down the opening in her shirt smearing his cum on her chest.

"You're so fucking hot." He bent, lifting her and putting her on the table before stepping between her legs. "How turned on are you?"

CHAPTER 5: SARAH

"Not at all." Sarah lied. She was almost ready to come. One touch of his longer fingers would probably send her over the edge but teasing him was so much fun. "Believe it or not, sucking your dick doesn't make me horny." She lied again. Having that control, that power over him made her hot and wet and needy.

"I don't believe it." His hand slowly made its way up her thigh.

"You should." She squeezed her legs together. It gave her some much needed pressure and trapped his hand between her legs.

"Maybe but I don't." He pulled free and grabbed her knees, forcing her legs apart.

"Stop. That's cheating." She laughed as she struggled against his strength.

"Is not. I kept my hands to myself during the blow job." He leaned closer, his hot breath tickling her ear. "It almost killed me, but I did it. For you."

"Not completely." She turned, drawn to him like the tide follows the moon.

His mouth came down on hers as his hand made its way up her leg. She moaned as his other hand grabbed her hair, pulling back her head and deepening the kiss. She clutched at his shoulders, unable to keep from touching him.

He pulled away, his lips a whisper from hers. "I'll ask again. How horny are you? And don't lie."

She scooted forward, trying to bring his hand to where she ached for his touch but his fingers danced aside, playing on her thigh.

"Tell me. How hot do you get sucking my dick?"

She could keep playing but his teasing touches were driving her mad and she was already so close. Sometimes it was better to surrender—much, much better. "Very. I need you to touch me. Please." She licked his lip.

"You like sucking my dick, don't you?" His long finger rubbed up and down her slit, getting wetter and slicker with each stroke.

"Yes." She needed more. More pressure, more friction. She grabbed his hand, pulling him to her pussy.

"Let go or I stop." He repeated the words she'd said to him.

"Ass." She almost hissed as she dropped her hand.

He laughed. "Maybe that is what I'll ask for when I win." He pulled her to the edge of the table, one of his fingers sliding to her butthole and teasing along the opening.

"Nick." She gasped. He usually stayed away from that area out of respect for her.

"I think you'll like it." He pulled his hand away and cradled her head as he lowered her back onto the table, his large body dwarfing her. His dick, no longer flaccid, bumped against her thigh. "I know I'll like fucking your ass." He kissed her and it was dark and deep, his tongue invading and conquering, making her combust with need. He pulled back, his lips brushing against hers with each word. "Should that be my prize?"

"I...I don't know." She was curious. Annie liked it and she trusted Nick not to hurt her.

"That's not a no."

"It's not a yes either." She still wasn't sure about anal.

"We'll table this discussion for later." He grabbed her legs, putting them straight up his chest. He guided his dick along her slit, teasing her. "You're so wet and hot."

"Please." She grabbed his wrist as she pressed into him. "I need you inside me."

"Then do it. You're in charge." He pulled her hand from his wrist, wrapping it around his cock.

She wasn't fooled for one second about being in charge, but with her hand around his dick she did have some control. She guided him to her entrance but couldn't move much because of her position. "Please, Nick."

He thrust forward and she gasped at his intrusion. "That's it." His one arm held her legs to his chest as he pulled almost all the way out before sliding back inside, filling her and stretching her, making her body pulse with his.

She reached for him but he was too far away so she grabbed the edge of the table as he rocked in and out, his pace slow and steady, but she needed faster and harder. She needed to come. "Please, Nick." She tried to rock with him but his arm held her in place.

"Not yet, baby."

"No. Please." She hated waiting. Playing and teasing was great for foreplay, but once his dick was buried inside her, it was time to fuck.

He shifted his stance as he stroked into her, his pace still slow but getting harder with each thrust. His other hand skimmed along her pussy, teasing her clit. Her body shook as she rocked her hips to rub against that wonderful finger.

"Not yet." He withdrew his hand.

"Damn it." She was done waiting for him. She reached between her legs. It felt better when he did it, but this would work too.

"Fuck, yeah. Touch yourself." His face took on an almost feral look and his pace increased, his thrusts harder and faster.

She spread her lower lips and stroked her pussy, making sure to gently scrape his penis with her nail every now and then.

"Fuck." He panted. "Now, who's...cheating?" He was fucking her hard now, his flesh slapping against hers.

"Yes. Nick. Yes." This was what she wanted. What she needed. She spiraled toward the finish.

His hand joined hers, his finger playing along her folds. "Keep touching your clit." His voice was like gravel as he slid in and out, harder and faster. "Shit. Sarah." He let go of her legs, his one hand teasing her clit while the other pinched her nipple.

Her eyes widened, locking with his as he fucked her. Sensations swirled through her. It was too much and not enough. Her body was ready to explode. She grabbed his hand, pressing down on her clit as her hips rocked, sending pain and pleasure ricocheting through her and pushing her over the edge. Her body bucked, tightening around him but he kept pumping into her, fast and hard. She screamed as another orgasm rocked through her.

"Shit." He grabbed her hips, his movements frantic now as he neared his release. He groaned as he exploded inside her. Her legs dropped to his sides as he braced himself on the table, lowering himself to kiss her. "I love you."

She ran her hands through his dark hair. "I love you too." She did and it scared the shit out of her. Everything was too good. It couldn't last. Good never did.

CHAPTER 6: SARAH

Sarah opened the back door. "Tank. Sweetie. Come." Both dogs looked at her and then back at the pool where Nick and the kids played. "You heard me. Get in here."

"You need to get your as…butt in here." Nick yelled from the pool. He held Davy, Maggie's two-year-old while Isabella, who was eight, and Peter, who was six, swam around him.

"Later. The pizza is—"

"Can the dogs stay here and play just a little longer?" Peter patted Sweetie as the pit-bull licked his face.

"No. They need to come in and—"

"Why?" asked Peter.

Between the two older kids it was almost impossible to finish a sentence without being interrupted by a question. "Tank's old and he needs to rest. Plus—"

"He doesn't look tired," said Isabella.

The Belgian Malinois was having the time of his life but he'd be hurting tomorrow if she didn't put a stop to his fun.

"No, he doesn't but he still needs to go inside and so do all of you. The pizza's here. Let's eat before it gets cold."

"I want to swim more. Please?" asked Isabella.

"Me too." Peter dived under the water, probably so he couldn't hear her.

"Please, Uncle Nick. Just five more minutes," begged Isabella.

"Peese Unca Nick." Davy clasped Nick's face with his chubby hands.

Sarah's heart almost burst with love and fear. "Tank. Sweetie. Come." She clapped her hands and the dogs trotted slowly toward her, heads down as if in trouble. Both of them kept glancing back at the kids. "Oh, stop it. I'll give you a cookie."

She closed the door behind the dogs and walked into the kitchen. Her phone rang and she grabbed it, as she handed the dogs each a dog cookie. "Hey Maggie, is everything okay?"

"That's what I'm calling to find out." Maggie laughed but there was a hint of tension in the sound. "It's not too late to change your mind. I haven't told Terry about his surprise yet."

"We wouldn't do that to you." Her friend had been planning this weekend for months.

"I know, but seriously, if you've changed your mind, I understand. Taking care of three kids is rough for one night. An entire weekend is…"

"We'll be fine."

"Are you sure?" Maggie's tone was hesitant. "Is Nick really okay with this?"

"Okay with it?" She laughed. "He's in heaven. He's in the pool, playing with the kids now. Are you sure you don't want to bring Beast over here? We can put him in a spare room away from our dogs and take turns letting him out with us and the kids."

"No thanks. He'll be happier at home, especially since Derek will be staying at the house."

"Derek?"

"The friend of Ethan's who's remodeling our bedroom."

"Oh, right. Nick hasn't talked about anything else since he heard about it."

"I can't believe Terry blabbed to everyone about that."

"Please. Those guys tell each other everything." Nick and his friends from La Petite Mort Club were all rich, handsome and the biggest gossips she'd ever met. "And now, Nick can't stop talking about starting a family. He's convinced himself that needing to be quiet during sex is the only way having kids disrupts a couple's sex life."

"Hardly." Maggie choked back a laugh. "I can't tell you how many times one of them ends up sleeping with us for some reason or other."

"I don't understand why he's in such a rush to get married and have kids." She sighed.

"Kids are great. I love mine dearly and wouldn't go back and change anything but don't have them if you're not ready."

"I won't. I may give in to Nick a lot but not on something like this."

"As for marriage…"

Sarah braced herself for the friendly intrusion into her life. Both Maggie and Annie were on Nick's side about the wedding.

"It has been awhile since you got engaged. I mean, don't rush it. If you aren't ready don't get married but…"

"I want to get married. I really do. I…There's so much to plan." It sounded lame even to her. She'd had plenty of time and she'd done nothing.

"Sarah…I…I hurried and got married. I loved David but…in hindsight, I should've waited. Lived a little."

"I've lived. It's not that." She was terrified that the good would end. It always did. Tank nudged her hand and she caressed his ear.

"Okay. Just know, I'll be here for you. No matter what." Maggie's voice cracked a little.

"Thank you." Great. Now, she was making Maggie relive her past and fears. When Maggie's ex had divorced her, she'd had no one. "I hope you know that I'll always be there for you too."

Maggie cleared her throat. "Thank you."

They'd met through their boyfriends but they were friends now and she meant it. Even if Terry and Maggie ended. She'd always consider the other woman as a friend.

"I'm going to ask one more time." There was a smile in Maggie's tone. "And if you say no, then that's it. The kids are yours for the weekend."

"I'm saying no. Go. Have fun at the Club."

"Okay." Maggie didn't hang up.

"You'll be fine. Just relax and follow Terry's lead. He'll love that."

"Yes, he does." Maggie sighed.

"And don't worry about the kids. We know how to find you if we need you."

"Sarah! I need your help," yelled Nick.

The kids' giggles spilled into the kitchen, making her gut twist with joy and fear. "I better go. You two have fun at the Club." She hung up the phone wishing she and Nick were going to the Club instead of babysitting. Sex was easy. Love and kids, family and life were terrifying.

He'd been great with the kids. Sure, it'd only been a few hours, but the way he played with them and talked to them made her heart wish for children of their own. He'd be a fabulous dad but she'd be a mess of a mother. She was still neurotic about crowds and the future and so many other things. She was working on her issues but she wanted her kids' lives to be perfect, not weighed down by their mother's baggage.

"Help me." Nick crawled into the kitchen, all three kids clinging to him.

She burst out laughing. Isabella was stretched out on his back, her hands tangled in his wet hair. Davy clung to his neck and Peter hung half on Isabella and half to the side. To top it off, Sweetie followed along, alternating between licking his face and then one of the kids. Basically, anyone who got near his tongue got a spit bath. She had no idea how Nick was able to move, let alone crawl.

"Laughing isn't helping." He shot her a stern look but his dark eyes were filled with humor. "Or maybe it's time for a counterattack." He grabbed Davy, tickling his chubby sides. The baby's screams of laughter echoed through the house.

"Get him, Peter." Isabella, not one to be left out, jumped off Nick's back and tried to help her baby brother.

"Hey, I was your horse. Your loyal steed." Nick put Davy on the floor and grabbed her, poking her sides. "You'll pay for this."

"Help. Get him. Tickle him," yelled Isabella as she squirmed and giggled.

Sarah didn't even have time to blink before Davy was shoving at Peter and trying to climb onto Nick.

"Sarah, help. I'm being overrun." He rolled to his back, the kids clambering over him.

She winced as Peter stood, his little foot landing right between Nick's legs.

"Ouch, fu—"

"Nick! The kids."

"I know." He said through gritted teeth, as he clutched his privates. "Time out."

"Uncle Nick needs a break." She grabbed Peter and Davy. "Isabella. Stop."

Nick rolled to a sitting position, still protecting his man parts.

"What's the matter?" asked Peter.

"You did it again." Isabella frowned at her brother.

"Daddy Terry told you to be careful where you put your feet."

"He's done this to Terry?" muttered Nick.

"All the time." Isabella nodded.

"Jesus. Someone could've warned me."

"I'm sorry, Uncle Nick. I didn't mean to step on your…"

Sarah's eyes met Nick's as her hand clamped over the child's mouth.

"Let him say it." He smirked through his grimace. "I know how Terry refers to *it* at the Club and I'm dying to know what he calls…*it* at home."

"I don't think that's a good idea." Terry was the crassest man she'd ever met. She wasn't sure she was ready to hear cock, or prick or dick come from such innocent lips as Peter's.

"Come on. I want to tease him at the Club," said Nick.

"About what?" asked Isabella.

Peter wiggled in Sarah's arms so she moved her hand. Smothering a child wasn't a good way to prove to herself that she'd make a decent mother.

"About where Daddy Terry"—Nick smirked again—"doesn't want Peter to step."

"You mean his pee-pee?" Isabella stared at Nick curiously. "Why would you tease him about that?"

"No reason. There's no reason at all to tease *Daddy* Terry about his *pee-pee*." Nick tried not to grin as his eyes met Sarah's. "I can't wait to go to the Club."

"Okay. Now that you've made Uncle Nick's night,

let's have some pizza." She put the two boys down.

Davy ran to Nick, crawling onto his lap and making himself comfortable.

"I'm not hungry." Isabella's lip jutted out. "I want to play horse again...in the pool."

"Maybe later." She grabbed the pizza boxes from the counter and placed a small slice on a plate. "Right now, it's time to eat. Then, maybe you can go swimming again."

"Yeah!" shouted Isabella and Peter.

Davy giggled, snuggling in Nick's arms.

Nick stood, carrying Davy to the table. "Don't we have to wait after we eat."

"No. That's only true if you're swimming for exercise. They'll be fine." She put the plate on the table in front of Davy.

"You have to cut it for him," said Isabella as she sat on a chair.

"Oh. Right." She should've known that. She'd seen her sister take care of Kyle but she'd never done it. Not when he'd been a baby. She grabbed the plate and walked back to the counter.

Nick came up behind her, running his hand down her back as he tossed two slices of pizza on two different plates. "It's no big deal," he said softly before kissing where her neck met her shoulder.

"I should've thought to cut the pizza. He could've choked."

"Nah. He just would've made a mess." His hand wandered across her lower back. "It's fine. You're doing great."

"No. You're doing great. I'm a wreck." She wiped at her eyes. She was going to be a horrible mother.

He captured her chin, forcing her to look at him. "This is new for both of us and we won't start with three older kids. We'll start with one baby and everything will be fine."

"I'm hungry," said Peter.

He kissed her again, soft and quick, before picking up the plates. "I got this and so do you."

CHAPTER 7: NICK

"Get your pajamas on and then we'll watch a movie." Nick ushered the two bigger kids into the guest room.

Sweetie shoved past him, not wanting to get left behind.

"Sweetie." Peter frowned at the dog, who wagged his tail and licked the boy's hand. "Be careful." He walked to the bed and started digging through his backpack, pulling out clothes, books and toys. "You almost knocked me over."

"Do you want me to dress Davy." Sarah stood at the end of the hallway. After dinner, they'd had fun in the pool but she was still a little shy, especially around the baby.

"No. I got him."

"Oh. Okay." Her face fell a little.

Okay. So, she wanted to do it. "Actually, why don't you take him." He was more than happy to hand the baby over to her. The whole purpose of this weekend was to show her that she could handle a baby. "And I'll get the movie started and make popcorn."

"Yeah!" shouted Isabella, quickly followed by her brothers' cheers.

"No. I'll do that. You can—"

He held Davy out to her and her eyes softened but the tension around her lips increased. "Sarah, it's better if you do it. I'm a man and I'm not going to be in the same bedroom with someone else's little girl while she changes."

"Nick, no one—"

"I know, but it's safer this way. Here." He thrust the baby into her arms. "You'll be fine."

"I've been around kids before, you know." She took the baby and smiled but it was tremulous.

No matter how many times she'd watched her nephew she obviously wasn't sure about being around a baby now. She stepped around him but he shifted, blocking her way.

He pulled her and Davy close. His hands, finally free of kids, grabbed her ass. "And later, I'll give you a present for being such a good surrogate mommy." His fingers trailed down her butt and between her legs. Her eyes darkened to an emerald green as he leaned in close, whispering. "If we were alone, I'd have you against the wall."

"Present?" Peter ran from the bedroom, pulling on his shirt. "I want a present. What are you going to give her, Uncle Nick? Can I have some? Will you share Aunt Sarah?"

"Go on, Nick. Tell Peter what you're going to give me." Her eyes sparkled with humor and he wanted her even more.

"A spanking." He swatted her ass and she squeaked.

"A spanking." Peter's voice filled with disgust. "That's not a present."

"It is if it's done right," he mumbled.

She laughed and pushed past him. "If that's the case, then maybe I'll give you a spanking."

"Not going to happen."

"It might when I win the bet."

"That's also not going to happen." He lunged, slapping her ass again.

"Hey. You'll pay for that." She hurried into the bedroom.

"Can't wait." *Good.* He'd used her tactics and diverted her nervousness with teasing and sex…or sexual innuendo. The sex would have to wait a few more hours, but that was fine. She was relaxed and confident. Now, he had to figure out how to help her be like that all the time, but it wouldn't happen overnight. Baby steps as Dr. Smileworth said. It was slow but it was progress.

"Come on." Nick held out his hand to Peter. "Help me make some popcorn."

"Hurry up, you two. I started the movie." Sarah walked into the kitchen as Nick added the butter to the big bowl of popcorn.

"Yeah!" Peter hopped off the chair that Nick had

placed near the counter.

"Wait." Nick handed him the bowl of popcorn. "Take this into the living room and share with your brother and sister."

"Okay." Peter walked carefully toward the door, trying not to spill a piece as Tank and Sweetie followed him, hoping he'd trip.

"Hurry, Aunt Sarah. Uncle Nick. The movie's starting," yelled Isabella.

"We'll be there as soon as I make some more popcorn." He poured some kernels into the air popper.

"You don't think that's enough for all of us?" asked Sarah. "It's huge."

"I do"—he grabbed her, pinning her against the counter—"but this gives us a few minutes alone." He kissed her, his tongue exploring her mouth as she melted against him. Her arms wrapped around his neck, causing her breasts to tease his chest. He had to get closer. He lifted her, pushing her legs apart and stepping between them, loving how she cradled his dick perfectly.

"The kids." Her hands ran through his hair.

"Are busy and we're just kissing."

"Really?" Her legs wrapped around him, pulling him closer and making his dick harden even more.

"Yeah. Until they go to sleep." His lips trailed down her neck to that spot where her shoulder met her neck. "Then you're mine and I expect an all-nighter. You owe me for abstaining."

"Abstaining?" She laughed but tipped her head giving

him better access. "We"—she glanced toward the living room—"did it in the morning and then twice before Maggie dropped off the kids."

"So." He cupped her breast through her shirt. "You know we would've done it more if they weren't here."

"More than three times before dinner? No. You're just horny because you know we can't." She moved his hand to her waist.

"Why isn't important." His hand trailed back up toward her breast. "I'm horn—"

"Aunt Sarah, I'm thirsty." Isabella stepped into the kitchen.

Sarah pushed on his chest but he wasn't moving that easily. He'd wanted to be in this position all day. They couldn't have sex but he could satisfy himself with a little groping.

"Nick. Move." She pushed on his chest again.

"Why? You know they've seen this before. They live with Terry for fu…goodness sake. Right Isabella?"

"What?" Isabella glanced into the living room, uninterested in what the adults were doing.

"You see Daddy Terry and your mommy kissing, don't you?"

"All the time." She sounded exasperated.

"Okaay, then." Sarah laughed.

"See. I told you." Nick squeezed her waist.

"I'm thirsty," repeated Isabella.

"Of course." Sarah tried to push away from him but he tightened his grip.

"There's soda in the fridge. Can you carry cans for you and your brothers?"

"Soda?" Isabella's eyes lit up. "And we all get our own can?"

"Sure." Nick's hand, that was blocked by Sarah's body, skimmed over her ass. "Why not?"

"Nick, I'm not sure. Maybe…"

"Thanks." Isabella hurried to the fridge, grabbing three cans of soda and running out of the kitchen.

"She seemed a little too excited about that." Sarah stared after her.

"Good. Excited is good." He was more than excited. He kissed down her neck, making his way to the cleavage displayed by her scoop necked T-shirt. Baring her breasts and worshiping them would have to wait, but he could tease and taste. He dipped his tongue between her breasts.

"Stop that." She tugged on his hair.

"Nope." He blew on her damp skin and she shivered, her thighs tightening around his.

"We can't finish. This is only making it worse."

"Nope again. This is much better." He pulled her flush against his cock. "I haven't dry humped in years. Takes me back. Makes me feel young."

"You spilled it," shouted Peter. "Uncle Nick, Isabella spilled the soda."

"I did not. It exploded."

Nick straightened, resting his forehead on hers. "Okay. Maybe the soda was a bad idea."

CHAPTER 8: SARAH

Sarah sat on the couch, leaning against Nick with Peter sprawled across both their laps. Isabella was stretched out on the floor between Tank and Sweetie. Davy was already in bed, having fallen asleep in Nick's arms halfway through the first movie. Her throat threatened to close at the memory—Nick so big and strong, cradling the sleeping child to his chest as he carefully made his way over Isabella, the dogs and Peter, who'd been on the floor by his sister at the time.

Her heart picked up speed. If she couldn't give him a child would he leave her? He should. He deserved kids of his own.

"You okay?" Nick whispered.

"Yeah." She turned toward him, plastering a fake smile on her face. The damn man must read minds because he always seemed to know when she was spiraling into panic.

His dark eyes studied her. She wasn't sure she could hide anything from him and she had to because she wasn't ready to face this fear. She glanced down as she ran her fingers through Peter's hair. It was dark and curly like Maggie's and so very soft. "It's just that this is…nice."

"Yes, it is but are you sure you're okay?" His hand skimmed up and down her arm.

"Yeah. He's so soft." She brushed some hair from Peter's cheek and he wiggled a bit. She was probably annoying the poor kid. She moved her hand to her leg. "Everything about kids is soft." She stared at the TV, seeing nothing but her memories. Her child had been so delicate. Fragile. The baby had needed her for everything and she'd failed.

"Not their feet."

"What?" Her gaze snapped to his.

Nick's eyes were filled with concern but a hint of humor sparkled in their dark depths. "Their feet aren't soft. At all. Especially, when they land on certain parts of your anatomy."

"I'm sure." She tried not to laugh.

"I'm positive." He frowned at her.

"I bet you are." She grinned and his eyes heated.

"Let's watch another movie," said Isabella.

"Can we?" Peter rolled over, his elbow catching Nick in the groin.

"Son-of-a…" He lifted Peter off his lap, dropping him onto Sarah's.

"Peter, be careful." Isabella frowned at them from the floor.

"What?" The little boy looked contrite but confused. "I

didn't do anything."

"You hurt Uncle Nick again."

Peter turned toward Nick. "Sorry." His eyes dropped to where Nick cupped himself. "I didn't mean to."

"It's okay, honey." She pulled him close, inhaling the smell of child—sunshine, chlorine from the pool and innocence.

"Easy for you to say," mumbled Nick.

"I...I didn't mean—"

"You have to be more careful," chided Isabella. "Daddy Terry said you have to watch where you put your feet and hands and—"

"Elbows and knees," Peter joined her.

"Jesus. He's a walking neutering machine," muttered Nick.

"And head." The two kids finished together.

"Head?" Nick looked horrified and Sarah covered her mouth with her hand, trying to stifle her laughter. "It's not funny." He glared at her. "How do...Your head? How is that even an issue?"

Isabella rolled her eyes. "He was running around the corner and ran right into Daddy Terry." Her little lips pursed. "He made Daddy Terry cry."

"I didn't mean to," whined Peter.

Sarah hugged him. "I know you didn't"—she kissed his head—"and so does Uncle Nick."

Nick frowned. "Mean to or not, it still hurts."

"Mommy kisses my owies and makes them better," said Peter.

Nick's eyes widened and Sarah's jaw dropped open.

"Maybe we can call her and she can kiss your owie, Uncle Nick," said Peter.

"No." Nick snapped and then his eyes gleamed. "Aunt Sarah can take care of that."

"You sure?" Peter turned on Sarah's lap and studied her.

"I'm positive." Nick grinned.

"But you don't have any kids," said Isabella.

"So?" Nick's eyes shifted to the little girl who stood in front of them.

"Only mommies can kiss it and make it better."

"That's true." Sarah smiled. "I guess Uncle Nick will have to kiss it himself."

"Don't think I wouldn't if I could," muttered Nick.

"Oh, I'm sure we'd never see any males if they could do that."

"Call Mommy," said Isabella. "She'll come over and help."

"Your mommy is busy tonight," said Sarah.

"I know what we can do." Peter wiggled on her lap, his elbow hitting her breast.

"Ouch." She grabbed her chest.

"See," whispered Nick.

"Call Uncle Nick's mommy," said Peter, oblivious to the pain he'd caused.

"Now, that's an idea." She struggled not to laugh at Nick's disgusted look.

"Yeah, a horrible one."

"Why Uncle Nick?" asked Peter.

"Yeah, Nick, why?" She bit her lip to keep from laughing when he sent her a you'll-pay-for-this look.

"Because"—his eyes gleamed with victory—"Aunt Sarah needs to practice."

"Why?" Isabella frowned up at him.

"She's going to be a mommy someday."

"Really?" Isabella's eyes dropped to Sarah's stomach. "You're having a baby?" She touched Sarah's flat belly. "If you're lucky, it'll be a girl." She glanced at her brother, shaking her head. "Boys are trouble."

Sarah would've laughed except Isabella's little hand on her belly sent panic shooting through her.

"Oh, she's not having a baby yet, but she will one day." Nick took her hand and her heart started to slow.

That's right. She wasn't pregnant now. She didn't have to worry about the hope, the love, the dreams building and then shattering in loss—millions of tiny shards of pain everywhere. Every breath. Every moment.

Nick's hand tightened on hers. "And before she does, she has to practice kissing owies and making them better."

"Hmm." Isabella didn't seem convinced.

"Girls aren't born knowing how to do that. They have to work at it." His eyes met Sarah's. "A lot."

She leapt at the opportunity to focus on his game—anything but her past. "You're impossible." Impossibly hot, sexy and hers. She loved this man more than was safe but he made her so horny that fear couldn't take root. All she wanted was to jump his bones. She'd be on him right now if the kids weren't here. Maybe this hadn't been such a good idea.

"I guess that makes sense," said Isabella. "I kissed Davy's boo-boo once when Mommy was busy in her room with Daddy Terry and it didn't help at all. He just kept crying until Mommy came out and got him."

Peter nodded. "Daddy Terry was grumpy."

"I bet." Nick smirked.

"What movie are we watching next?" Isabella grabbed the remote from the table.

"Next, is bedtime." Nick stood, snatching Peter from the couch.

"Please, one more," begged Peter.

"Nope. Time for bed." Nick started across the living room.

"They have to brush their teeth and go to the bathroom first." She didn't need wet beds.

"I'm hungry," said Peter.

"I'm not tired,' said Isabella.

"It's bedtime," said Nick.

"I'm starving." Peter clutched his belly. "Please."

"I need some water," said Isabella.

Nick stood in the middle of the room looking flummoxed.

Sarah had seen Maisie go through this with her nephew a million times. She could do this. "Peter, you had pizza and a ton of popcorn. You can wait until breakfast." She stood, turning toward Isabella. "You can have some water after you brush your teeth." She grabbed the little girl's shoulders and pointed her down the hallway. "Go. If you hurry, we'll let the dogs sleep in your room tonight but only if they want to."

"Yeah." Isabella ran down the hallway.

"But I'm not tired," whined Peter.

"You need to sleep." She walked over to them. "You don't want to be crabby tomorrow, do you?" She brushed the hair from his eyes. "We have a big day planned."

"We do?" Peter's eyes sparkled.

"Yes," Nick headed for the bathroom. "We're going to go for a picnic and to the zoo..."

Nick's voice grew softer as he walked into the bathroom. She stared after them, a slight smile on her face. Maybe she could do this after all.

CHAPTER 9: NICK

"The end," whispered Nick as he closed one of the books that Maggie had sent with the kids.

"Another one," said Peter.

"I've already read you two." He sat up. "It's time for bed."

"But we're not tired," said Isabella.

Davy snuffled in his sleep, turning in the playpen.

"Shhh." Nick crawled out from between the two kids. "Don't wake your brother."

"Another story. Please," begged Isabella. "Then we'll go to sleep. We promise."

"Tomorrow."

"Kisses," said Peter.

"That I can do." He leaned down, his heart turning to mush as the little boy's arms wrapped around his neck. "Good night." He kissed Peter on the cheek."

"Night, Uncle Nick." Peter tucked his stuffed bear in his arms and rolled over.

Nick walked to the other side of the bed. "Goodnight, Isabella."

"I should get to stay up later than Peter. I'm bigger." She stared up at him, eyes narrowed making her look decades older than eight.

"Well, you'd be up all alone because I'm going to bed." *Not to sleep, but to bed.*

"Is Aunt Sarah going to bed too?"

"Yes." She'd better be waiting for him, naked.

"Okay." Isabella hugged him, giving him a kiss on the cheek. "Good night, Uncle Nick."

"Night." He tucked the blankets around her and left the room. Sweetie hopped off the bed and followed him.

"Sweetie. I want him to sleep with us." She sat up.

He stopped in the doorway. "It's his choice. Call him and see if he wants to stay."

"Sweetie, come here." She patted the bed.

The dog looked from her to Nick.

"Go on, if you want." He nodded at the bed.

Sweetie wagged his tail but didn't move.

"Sweetie, come here." Peter started patting the bed and calling the dog.

"Shhh." He glanced at the playpen but Davy was still sound asleep.

Tank trotted into the room. He'd stayed with Sarah in the kitchen after the kids had gotten their water.

"Tank. Come here, boy," said Isabella.

Tank jumped on the bed, flopping between the kids. Sweetie hopped up beside him, stretching out alongside

Peter.

"Goodnight." He turned off the light.

"It's too dark," whined Isabella.

"Close your eyes. You won't notice it."

"I'm scared," said Peter. "Please, turn the light on."

"Okay." He flipped it back on. The two smiled at him, making him feel like a hero.

"Thank you," they both said.

"You're welcome. Now, get some sleep." Because it was time for him to get laid. He closed the door and headed down the hallway.

He stopped in the doorway of the kitchen. Sarah was sipping from a glass of wine as she emptied the dishwasher.

"Woman. Get that sexy ass into our bedroom." If the kitchen had a door, he'd fuck her right here against the counter.

"How many books did they get you to read?" She turned, closing the dishwasher and leaning against it.

"Two." He strolled toward her, his eyes roaming her slender frame.

"Only two? You did good." She sipped her wine, her eyes drifting over him in a slow caress that made his dick harden even more.

"I did." He closed the distance, his arms wrapping around her. "You ready to concede?"

"Hardly." She laughed, her hands caressing their way up and down his chest. "The night is young and the weekend is younger."

"I get better with practice." He pulled her against him.

"You can attest to that."

"Yes. You had plenty of practice before I met you." Her arms circled his neck, her fingers sliding through his hair. She kissed him, tasting of wine and popcorn and her. He pulled her closer, rocking against her.

"I want to take you right now. Right here." His hand cupped her breast. "So, we'd better move to the bedroom before I lose the little control I have."

"We'd better." She kissed him again. "Because I've been waiting all night."

"You have?" He leaned back, his hands on her ass.

"Yep. Apparently, I need practice." Her eyes sparkled with humor.

"Practice?"

"Kissing it and making it better."

"Oh, you do." He lifted her in his arms. "You certainly do and I know the owie you can practice on." He strode toward their room.

"I'm going to start here"—she nipped his lip and then ran her tongue over it—"and move down your body." She kissed her way to his ear and whispered, "I'll use my teeth. Not too hard but enough to give you a boo-boo and then I'll kiss it and make it all better." Her tongue darted into his ear and he stumbled. "Hey." Her arms tightened around his neck.

"You may have to postpone that until round two." He closed the door behind him and pressed his dick against her, letting her feel how ready he was.

"Nope. You said I needed to practice so you're going

to have to suffer through it."

"You're an evil woman." He took two more steps into the room and tossed her on the bed. "And I'm a hero." He spread his arms. "I conquer evil." He launched himself at her.

She squealed, rolling to her side but he was on top of her before she could get away. He grabbed her shoulder, throwing her onto her back. "You're mine, evil woman." He held her hands at the sides of her head.

"What are you going to do, Mr. Hero? Bang the bad out of me?"

"Hell, yes"—he laughed as he grabbed both her hands in one of his and reached between them—"and I think this first time you need it hard, really hard."

"I think, I need to be naked for that punishment."

"I agree." His humor fled as he let go of her hands so she could wiggle out of her pants. He barely waited for her to kick them off her feet before his hand slid between her legs. She was wet and ready for him. "I need you." He kissed her, sinking his finger into her pussy as his tongue explored her mouth. She was so hot for him, always.

Her hands went to his pants, undoing his button before moving to his zipper. He kissed her neck, teasing that spot she loved with his tongue and teeth before sucking on it. She moaned, squeezing his cock but the damn zipper was still up.

"Sarah, stop playing around." When she didn't respond, he pushed her hand out of his way and lowered his zipper. His dick needed to be free and then inside her.

"Wait. Shhh." She moved her head, staring over his shoulder.

"What?" His dick rested on her mound, impatient to get going.

"Don't you hear that?"

"Hear what?" All he could hear was his blood roaring through his body.

"The kids."

"They're asleep." *They'd better be fucking asleep.*

"They are not asleep. They're playing." She pushed at his chest, but he wasn't going anyway.

"No. They aren't." He could hear the giggles now and he wanted to cry. "They're asleep." He ran his finger along her seam, teasing around her clit. "I don't hear anything and neither do you."

A loud laugh echoed through the house.

"We can't." She stuck her hand between her legs, cock blocking him.

"Fuck, Sarah." He shot her a glare as he rolled off her.

"We can't ignore it. They'll get louder and more excited."

He was going to cry. His balls would turn blue and he'd cry.

"We have to stop it now, or they won't sleep for hours." She started to get out of bed.

He pushed her back down and was on her again, back between her legs but not inside her body. "I'll go. You wait here." He kissed her hard and fast and then rolled to the side, pulling up his pants. "I want you naked, legs spread and waiting for me when I get back." He strode from the room, his dick protesting the scrape of his clothes with every step.

CHAPTER 10: NICK

Nick quietly opened the bedroom door. The two kids sat on the bed while Tank and Sweetie stood on the floor, staring at them expectantly. Both dogs glanced at him and then looked right back at the kids.

"It's my turn," said Peter.

"Tank brought it to me." Isabella held one of Davy's toys in her hand. "You don't throw good." She tossed it across the room.

The dogs bounded after it.

"I do too. I throw better than you." Peter's face scrunched up in anger.

He was stopping this argument before it really got going—just like the little brats had stopped him. "What are you doing?" He fought back a laugh as both of them jumped like scared cats and then flopped back on the bed, closing their eyes.

"Please. I saw you."

They kept their eyes shut.

"I know you're not sleeping." It was insulting how stupid they thought he was.

"We are," whispered Peter.

"Peter." Isabella's tone dripped with disgust.

"What?" Peter's eyes popped open.

"Enough." He had a hot, horny woman naked and waiting for him.

They both looked at him, their little eyes wide.

"I told you to go to sleep." He strode into the room, his mind scrambling for something else to say. What had he hated hearing as a child? "I'm so disappointed in both of you. I thought you were a big boy and girl who did what you were told."

"Sorry." Peter's lip jutted out a bit.

"But we're not tired." Isabella stared at him, a challenge in her hazel eyes.

He was going to have to pull out the big guns. "Tank. Sweetie. Go." He pointed out the door. "Go to bed."

"No," cried Isabella as the dogs lowered their heads and trotted toward the door. "You said they could sleep with us."

"You aren't sleeping and you're not tired." He wanted to pat himself on the back.

"We'll go to sleep. We promise," said Peter.

"Sorry. I don't think I can trust you anymore." This had killed him as a kid.

Tank stopped in the doorway, Sweetie right behind him, and gave a longing look at the bed.

Nick raised his hand. "Go."

The dogs slowly walked into the hallway as if their legs were weighed down with bricks.

"No. Please, please." Isabella got on her knees, clasping her hands together. "I'll go to sleep. I promise."

"But you're not tired."

"I am now." She forced a fake yawn.

He couldn't stop one side of his mouth from quirking upward. "You promise?"

"Yes." She nodded.

"Okay."

"Tank. Sweetie." She patted the bed.

The dogs looked at him.

"Go ahead." He pointed at the bed and the dogs, suddenly free from the bricks around their legs, raced into the room. Tank jumped on the bed but Sweetie went right for the toy. Nick snapped his fingers and the dog brought it to him. He dropped it on the dresser, ignoring the dog's expectant look. "Now, go to sleep."

"Okay." Isabella dropped to her back next to her brother, eyes shut, her hand stroking Tank's fur.

He closed the door and waited. It barely took a minute before soft whispers drifted into the hallway. He opened the door and Peter dropped back down on his pillow.

"If either of you talk or sit up again, the dogs leave. Understand?"

"Yes, sir," they said in chorus.

He closed the door again and waited. Nothing but silence. He waited a little longer. Still nothing. Thank God. All he could think about was Sarah, lying naked, legs spread, pussy wet and waiting for him. He hurried back to their bedroom, his cock rising again for the occasion.

CHAPTER 11: SARAH

Sarah pulled off her shirt, tossing it onto the floor before leaning against the headboard. She was so wet and aching for Nick.

He'd never been sexier than when he'd been playing with the kids and her womb had practically wept when he'd held Davy's little body so carefully in his large hands as he carried the baby to bed.

Her head balked at the idea of getting pregnant but her body wanted him and their baby. Not yet. After they married. But not too long after. Sweat broke out across her skin. She couldn't risk it. She couldn't go back to before— alone, scared, so sad she could barely function. She'd never survive that again. She'd barely survived it the first time.

She went into the bathroom, turned on the faucet and splashed cold water on her face. It didn't have to be like last time. Nick wasn't Adam and even if he left, she'd survive. She was strong but then the memories rushed her, coming from all directions. The fear and pleasure when she'd realized she was pregnant. Eager to tell Adam but he hadn't loved her. He'd fallen for someone else. The pain. Her heart broken. The death. The blood. The loss. She wrapped her arms around her stomach as the emptiness and ache of those days so many years ago hit her like a punch, knocking the breath from her chest. She put her head between her legs and took deep, breaths.

She had to calm down. If Nick found her like this, he'd never let up until she confessed everything and then…then he'd understand, or at least say he did but it'd be different between them. He'd treat her more carefully, as if she'd break, and she'd feel that way—like porcelain, ready to crack at the slightest bump.

She'd bring up having kids again in her sessions with Dr. Smileworth. She'd step up her meditation and exercises to work through these things. She didn't have to do anything right now and, if she were lucky, after this weekend, Nick might drop the topic of kids for a while. Her heart slowed. He sure hadn't been happy about having to stop mid-penetration. He'd probably never been interrupted in his life.

She stood, red eyes staring back at her. This wasn't going to work. The damn man was too observant. She wet a washcloth and wiped her face, removing her makeup and making sure the redness around her eyes was gone. She turned on the warm water and then ran the cloth over her body.

She went back into the room and climbed on the bed. He still wasn't back. Maybe she should see if he needed help. She hopped out of bed, pulling on her robe. She opened the door and heard him telling the kids that the dogs would go if they didn't behave. He seemed to have it under control. She moved back to the bed and hesitated, grinning as she opened her nightstand and pulled out her vibrator.

CHAPTER 12: NICK

Nick's froze right outside his bedroom door. He knew that sound. It was a man's worst nightmare. He loved using the vibe with Sarah in bed but to have her start without him…Fuck that. He threw open the door and all the blood rushed to his pounding cock.

She sat naked with her back against the headboard, and her legs spread as she slid the vibrator across her pussy. Her chest heaved and her skin was covered in a rosy hue. Her eyes locked with his, gleaming forest green in the dim light from the lamp near the bed. "You're late."

"Give it to me." He closed the door and held out his hand as he walked to the bed, undoing his jeans.

"No." She shifted, letting the tip of the toy slip inside her body.

"Fuck." It should be him sliding inside her. In a minute it would be. He shoved his pants down, kicking them off and then crawled across the bed. He grabbed her wrist, stopping her from pleasuring herself.

"Let go." She yanked but his grip was firm. "It feels so good." She licked her lips. "Please, don't make me stop, Master."

His balls tightened. This wasn't going to take long. He wasn't in the mood for games, not now, but this was one of his favorites. His lips hovered a fraction above hers. "I can make you feel better."

"Hmm. I don't.—"

"Trust me." He moved his hand that held her wrist, brushing the toy right below her clit.

She let go of the vibrator as his lips met hers, devouring her. He pulled her downward, spreading her legs wider as his hot cock slid along her wetness. She was so slick and ready. Her body trembled beneath his, already almost at orgasm. Her arms wrapped around his shoulders and her legs over his, pulling him closer, pulling him to her opening.

A sharp bark rang through the air followed by giggles and then loud whispers.

"Be quiet," said Isabella.

"Sorry," said Peter.

"You said they were sleeping." Sarah shoved at his chest. She was as unhappy about this as he was. "Get off me."

"Wait." He pressed down harder on her, holding her in place. He couldn't bring himself to move, not with his dick so close to heaven.

"Why? You know they'll just get louder."

"They aren't really doing anything bad." He shifted,

reaching between them. "This will only take a few minutes."

"You want to…. While they're playing in the other room loud enough to wake the baby."

She hadn't said no.

He shrugged, running the tip of his cock through her wetness. "We could be done quick." He kissed her ear. "You could sleep and I'll go take care of them." He slid inside her just a little. Her pussy clamping around him, welcoming him and inviting him deeper.

Another bark, this time followed by a loud crash.

"Shit." Even he knew it was over but he thrust inside her all the way, loving how she gasped. His hips pumped twice before he rolled to the side, pulling from her body.

"Nick." Her hand clasped his arms, her fingernails digging into his skin.

"I got it," he said through clenched teeth.

"Be quick."

He pulled on his pants, wincing as he tried to zip them. Instead he grabbed a business shirt from the chair.

"What are you doing?" Her fingers skimmed over her abdomen, getting closer and closer to her pussy.

"Covering the bulge in my pants." He buttoned the bottom part of the shirt before leaning down, grabbing her hands and sucking her fingers. "Don't start without me. I'll be right back."

"Make sure they're asleep this time." She frowned at him.

"Don't worry. I will." He strode down the hallway.

"Either that or I'm going to tie them to the bed and gag them."

CHAPTER 13: NICK

"Holy shit, that took forever," Nick muttered as he closed the door to the room where the kids were finally asleep. The only thing keeping him from running across the house to his bedroom was the way his luck was going. Tonight, he'd probably trip and bust his head and then he'd never get laid.

He walked into the room, closing the door behind him. "Sorry. Those little buggers would not go to sleep." He pulled off his shirt as he headed toward the bed, shoving his pants down and flopping onto the mattress. "Now, where were we?" He burrowed under the covers. "Oh, that's right. I was about to fuck…"

A soft snort came from Sarah followed by the sound of steady breathing.

"No." He grabbed her shoulder. "Sarah, honey. Are you asleep?" He knew damn well she was sleeping but right now he didn't care. He shook her. "Wake up." He pulled her against him, her naked body fitting almost perfectly with his. The one thing that'd make it better was his dick buried inside her. He kissed her neck and she sighed. He could work with that. His hand trailed down her stomach and between her legs. She was still slick from earlier. He nibbled her ear. "Wake up, baby. We have some unfinished business." His finger slipped inside her but she continued to breathe slow and steady, no hitch, no movement. She was out cold. "Fuck." He rolled onto his back. "Only a jerk would fuck a woman who was sleeping, right?" He said it loud and clear, maybe a little louder than he needed to. "I mean, we are in a relationship and you did want it." He leaned up on his elbow, brushing some hair from the side of her face. "It's not like we were fighting or anything." He poked her, none too gently between the shoulder blades. "You might even wake and enjoy it. Right?" He shook her shoulder. "How about this? If you want me to stop, you tell me. Okay?"

A soft snore drifted across the room.

He dropped onto his back, spitting into his palm before wrapping it around his cock. "Fuck me." He hadn't jerked off since she'd been at the clinic. "The least you can do is give me a show." He yanked the covers off her and hope flared in his chest as she rolled onto her back, but it crashed and died. She was still sound asleep.

His eyes raked over her body as he stroked his cock. Her breasts were perfect and they were so soft, even her nipples were like velvet. His mouth watered, begging him for a taste but that'd be wrong. Although, he wouldn't care if she fucked him while he was sleeping. No. He couldn't, not without talking to her about it first. How had they never discussed this? He increased his pace, his hand sliding up and down his cock, a poor substitute for her pussy, or mouth, or even her hand. Fuck him. This sucked but tonight all he had was a peep show of his sleeping fiancé.

She shivered, curling in a ball for warmth.

"Damn it." He sat up, pulling the blanket around her. "I don't even fucking get that." He got out of bed and walked into the bathroom for a cold shower.

CHAPTER 14: SARAH

Sarah rolled over and opened her eyes. The room was dark except for a small bit of sunlight that crept through the curtains. Nick had left to get the kids to go to sleep but his large body was stretched out next to her. Damn, she must've fallen asleep waiting for him. She bit her lip to keep from laughing at how pissed he must've been when he'd found her sleeping. Pissed and horny. Her eyes roamed over his back—all that smooth, warm skin just waiting for her hands. The house was still quiet. They had time before the kids woke. She leaned up, resting her head on one of her hands while the other one skimmed across his back. "Hey, you awake?" She leaned closer and kissed his shoulder.

His breathing stayed steady.

She let her hand wander down to his ass as she shifted closer to press against his side. She kissed his neck. "The kids are sleeping but they'll probably wake soon." She let her tongue slip inside his ear and then blew softly. "Wake up if you wanna fuck."

He snored softly.

"Damn." It was time to rev this up a notch. She had a sexy, naked guy in her bed. She did not want to masturbate. That was it. That sound might filter through his sleep. "Okay. I guess, I'll start without you again." She nipped his earlobe, a little harder than she normally would but these weren't normal circumstances.

He snuffled, turning his head away.

She rolled over, grabbed her vibrator from the nightstand where she'd put it last night. "I'm not kidding. You're going to be upset when I'm no longer in the mood." She turned on the vibrator. She wasn't happy that she was back to this. Using it with him was fun, but by herself? No. She'd much rather have his cock. She lowered the toy between her legs, stroking it gently across her pussy. "Mmm. This is nice," she said louder than necessary. The damn man had better wake up because it did feel good and she was extremely horny. She spread her legs, slipping the toy between her folds and shivering a little at the vibrations. She closed her eyes, imagining Nick above her, holding her down as he used the vibe on her. Her breath came quicker as she lost herself to the fantasy. She jumped as a hand wrapped around her wrist.

"Not this time." He pulled her to him, throwing her leg over his hip and sliding inside her in one hard thrust. "Good morning." He kissed her, it was slow and gentle but filled with heat.

"Morning." She tightened around him, making his eyes

burn with desire.

"You fell asleep last night." He pumped into her, his rhythm slow and steady.

The evenings were for games and teasing but the mornings were different. A slow burn. Just her and him together in pleasure. Her hands skimmed over his strong cheek bones and then into his thick, soft hair.

"I know. Sorry." Her breath hitched as his hands grabbed her ass pulling her into his thrust. "You should've woken me."

"I tried." He rolled her over, pinning her beneath his strength and pumping harder and faster. "Believe me, I tried." He nipped her ear. "I almost fucked you anyway."

"You…"

A cry burst through the house.

"Davy," she moaned.

"No. Fuck. No." But he pulled from her, rolling to his back.

She gasped as he left her. Her body clenching on nothing. Denied again. "Damn it. We should've moved faster."

His arm was over his eyes, his chest rising and falling as if he'd run a marathon. His face was hard and so was his cock, the tip purple and angry looking.

"I got him." She got out of bed, putting on her robe. "You should…"

He shifted his arm and looked at her with one eye. "I should what?" He wasn't amused.

"Finish." She waved her hand near his dick. "I won't

be back."

"What?" Now, he was more than unhappy.

"The kids will wake and there's no way we're getting Davy back to sleep anyway."

"Fuck." He pulled the pillow over his face and screamed.

CHAPTER 15: NICK

Nick was not going another evening without sex. He was an adult. They were kids. He'd win this war. He'd planned the day to perfection. He'd exhaust the kids and when they passed out, he and Sarah could fuck like rabbits because once was not going to be enough.

"Maybe we should take them home." Sarah started gathering the leftover food from the picnic and putting it away.

"No. Not yet."

"But they're tired."

Davy sat in the middle of the playground rubbing his eyes while Peter chased Isabella, crying because she wouldn't let him catch her.

"Not tired enough." The two were still running for God's sake.

"They're crabby and fighting." She stuffed more food in the cooler. "We should've gone home after the zoo and let them nap."

"Why so they can interrupt us again?"

"Shhh." She glanced at the other couples but no one seemed to have heard him.

"Sorry." He wasn't. It was the truth and every guy here would agree with him.

"We need to get them home and let them wind down."

"That is absolutely not going to happen. Then they'll be recharged and ready to go all night." He shook his head. "Not again. I'm not having another night like last night." His balls couldn't take it.

"Nick..."

"Nope." He kissed her. "Trust me. We'll leave soon. Then we can bathe them, feed them and put them to bed." He kissed her again. "And then we can go to bed, but right now it's time for tag."

"Nick, don't."

He ignored her and headed for the playground.

"Good luck with that," said a guy as he passed.

"With what?"

"Kids. Tag. And"—he glanced behind him—"alone time."

Nick stopped.

"Sorry. Couldn't help over hearing you."

"Yeah. No problem." He hadn't exactly been whispering. He took another step and stopped. "Why don't you think it'll work?"

"Kids get too tired." The stranger frowned, shaking his head. "And that's never good."

"Why? Do they get sick or something?" He didn't

want them sick or hurt. He just wanted them to sleep so he could get laid.

"Nah. Not really but they do get crabby and then she gets crabby and…it doesn't work."

"You tried it?"

"Oh yeah." The man glanced behind him again at a pretty blonde holding a baby. "She's my second wife." He pointed to the playground at two blonde boys about six years old. "Those two are her kids. The baby is mine."

"Congratulations." He wanted that but then they grew into cock blockers. He shot a glare at Maggie's kids.

"Thanks. I'd suggest you let them take a little nap and get some rest."

"Yeah? That didn't work too well last night."

The guy shrugged. "Just saying. Getting them overtired doesn't work either."

"I'll keep that in mind." He almost rolled his eyes. This guy must not have done it right. The dumbass probably let his wife sway him into not pushing them to the point of exhaustion.

"Suit yourself." The guy shook his head.

"Gotta run." Nick nodded to the guy as he continued toward the playground. He had nieces and nephews. He knew how to tire out kids. "Hey, Isabella, Peter. Grab your little brother and let's play tag."

"Yeah!" shouted Isabella.

"Are you a zombie?" asked Peter as he barreled across the lot.

Nick quickly turned, cringing as Peter's head hit his

leg but it was a hell of a lot better than his nuts. "Yeah." He moaned like a zombie. "I'm a zombie."

"Arghh." Peter ran away.

Nick staggered after the kids, hands out and moaning. "Dumb ass."

"Hey." He glanced at the man who'd been talking to him.

The guy shook his head as he gathered his kids to leave.

CHAPTER 16: SARAH

By the time they got home Sarah was ready to kill all of them, especially Nick. Not only had he run the kids ragged but then he'd filled them up with soda and ice cream at McDonalds. Now, the kids were being crabby little shits. She stuffed the leftovers from the restaurant into the fridge.

"Uncle Nick, Isabella is touching me," whined Peter.

"Am not." Isabella had her hand right next to, but not touching, her brother's face.

Nick held Davy who was fighting sleep. "She's not actually—"

"Isabella, go get in the shower." She'd had enough of all of them.

"Why me?"

"You're all going to shower—"

"But why do I have to go first? It's not fair." Isabella ran her hand down her brother's face before folding her arms across her chest.

"See. See. She touched me," shouted Peter as he

96

tugged on Nick's arm.

Sarah took a deep breath. "Isabella, you'll be the first done and then you can help me in the kitchen."

"Doing what?" The little girl eyed her suspiciously.

"Uhm. Getting your snack ready." Not like they hadn't had enough goodies for the night...or week.

"What kind of snack?" asked Peter.

"Cookies," said Nick as he put the sleeping Davy on the couch. "Sarah's going to make cookies."

"Cookies?" She sent Nick a glare that could wither a stone.

"Yeah." He smiled, oblivious to how close to death he was.

"Then I guess you're going to the store to get the ingredients."

"Oh. Sure. What do we need?"

"Forget it." She turned to the kids. "We're not having cookies."

"But I want cookies," said Peter.

"You promised," said Isabella.

"Hey, wake up." Nick gently shook the baby.

"I did not promise and you"—she turned toward Nick—"stop trying to wake him."

"But he needs to sleep...later." His eyes raked over her body.

"You wake that baby and there'll be no reason for him to sleep later."

Nick's brow wrinkled and his eyes darkened. "The reason will be invalid if he sleeps now."

"He's a baby. He needs his rest."

"And he'll get it." He glanced at the other two who were arguing over who got to sit by Sweetie. "Later."

"Stop fighting over the dog." She grabbed Peter's hand. "Go with Uncle Nick and take a bath."

"Me?" Nick pointed to himself

"But I don't want to take a bath," said Peter

"Too bad." She gave him a gentle push toward Nick.

"Ha, ha. Peter has to take a bath," said Isabella.

She spun around. "And so do you, young lady."

"Mommy said we're too old to take baths together." Isabella had a superior look on her little face that made Sarah want to scream.

"We have two bathrooms." She almost grinned as Isabella's smug look turned to surprise and then pouting.

"I don't want to use the other bathroom. I want to use the one Peter is using."

"I don't give a—"

"Isabella." Nick stepped forward and bent in front of the little girl so they were eye level. "Maybe if you're good, Sarah will let you use some of her soap that makes her smell so good."

"Really?" Isabella looked up at her, the bratty expression replaced by the face of an innocent angel.

"If you're good." Right now, she'd promise almost anything to get the kids to stop bitching. If she could, she'd drop the kids off at the Club with their mother but that wasn't an option. She'd agreed to this—lord help her—and she'd see it through.

"Okay." Isabella stood and took Sarah's hand.

"Why does she get to use your bathroom," whined Peter. "I want to use your bathroom too."

"Maybe tomorrow." Nick took his hand and led him down the hallway.

Tomorrow? They'd better not be bathing the kids again. If Maggie didn't get here early those kids might be locked in one of the dog cages. She had several waiting in the garage to be delivered to foster families who'd agreed to take in one of the rescues from her business.

CHAPTER 17: NICK

Nick wrapped Peter in a towel as he lifted the child from the tub. "Let's get you dressed."

"Okay." Peter put his arms around Nick's neck, resting his head on his shoulder.

Nick's heart twisted. God, he wanted one of these. Yes, he hadn't had sex in more than twenty-four hours but their kids would be different. He'd teach them from a young age to go to bed when told and sleep through the night. He put Peter down on the toilet seat and grabbed the kid's pajamas.

"I don't want to go to bed." Peter wrapped his arms around his chest, refusing to give Nick his arm.

"You're not going to bed." He wasn't done tiring them out yet. When he was, they'd sleep like the dead and he'd fuck like a king.

"Then why do you have my pajamas?"

"Because"—he tried to pry one of Peter's arms loose but the kid was stronger than he looked—"I thought we could watch movies again like last night. You'd like that, right?"

"Yes." Peter nodded.

"Great, but you have to get dressed." He waved the pajama top. "So, lift your arms."

"I want to wear my Spider-Man shirt."

"This has Batman on it." He showed the boy the shirt.

"I want Spider-Man."

"Okay." He didn't give two shits what the kid wore as long as he fell asleep—soon. He grabbed the backpack and dug through it. "Uhm. Do you know where your Spider-Man shirt is?"

"Uh-huh." Peter nodded.

Nick waited and waited, the muscle in his jaw starting to do the cha-cha. "Where? Where is it?"

"Dirty."

Nick thought back. "You wore a shirt with trains on it yesterday."

Peter nodded. "But I want Spider-Man."

"You wore these pajamas last night and a Hulk T-shirt today."

"Spider-Man."

"Where is that shirt?" He dug in the bag again.

"It's dirty." Peter's tone was disgusted. The kid didn't say I told you so, but he may as well have.

He turned to the hamper but it was empty. "Do you know what Aunt Sarah did with it?" She may have washed it already.

"No." Peter shook his head. "Mommy has it not Aunt

Sarah."

"Mommy? How…It's at your house, isn't it?" He wanted to slap his head.

"Uh-huh."

His teeth ground together as he lifted the pajamas and snatched Peter's arm that was no longer tight against his chest. "Well, we can't go to your house tonight, so these will have to do."

"No." Peter tried to pull his arm free, but Nick tightened his grip, shoving the kids arm through the hole. "I want Spider-Man."

"Tomorrow." After his damn mother came and picked him up.

"Now." Peter's eyes welled with tears.

"Tomorrow." He pulled the shirt over the boy's other arm and down past his head. "Stand up."

"I want my mommy." Peter's lower lip trembled.

"I want your mommy too." He lifted the kid and slid the pajama bottoms up his legs.

"I hate you."

"Good." He wasn't too fond of the boy right now either. "Now, let's go watch a movie."

"No. I don't want to." Peter shoved at Nick's chest.

"Then, you go to bed."

"No." Peter glared at him.

"Yes." He was not negotiating with the little terrorist.

"No."

"Yes." One more *no* and he'd toss the brat into the bedroom, locking the door behind him.

"Nick…" Sarah stood in the doorway. "Is everything okay?"

She was his beautiful angel, his salvation. He wanted to wrap his arms around her and just hold her. These kids were monsters, but the two of them were a team. "He wants his Spider-Man shirt that's at his house and he hates me."

"He's overtired." She sent him an I-told-you-so look.

So much for being in this together. Somehow, even though he wasn't the one who'd volunteered to watch them, this was all his fault.

"He should've taken a nap." She didn't have to say, *like I told you*, because it was clear in her narrowed gaze and tightness around her mouth.

But he was right about wearing them out. "Speaking of that, is Davy still sleeping?"

"Yes. I put him in his playpen."

He was going to throttle her but first… "Peter, you can either watch a movie with us, or you can go to bed."

"I want Spider-Man."

"Bed it is." He picked him up.

"No. Movie. Movie." Peter clung to Nick, half choking him.

"Okay." He gasped as he lowered the boy to the floor, prying Peter's hands free. "Go. Get your seat."

"I call couch." Peter ran from the room.

Sarah bent and grabbed the towel.

Nick couldn't help it. His hand went to her ass like a magnet to lead.

"Don't." She straightened

"Don't what?" He moved closer. "It's been hours since I've kissed you."

"And it'll be more." She sidestepped him.

"Why? They're quiet. We have a few minutes."

"No, we don't."

"Yes. We do." He grabbed her, pulling her into his arms and kissing the top of her head.

"Nick, stop." She struggled but he held her tighter. "I have to clean the bathroom. The floor's soaking wet. There's soap every—"

"I'll get it later." His hands cupped her ass.

"It needs to be done before the kids slip and fall."

"I'll get it."

"When?"

His jaw clenched. "I do my share around here. I'm not some lazy ass who expects his woman to do everything."

"I know. I'm sorry. It's…" She sighed, resting her head on his shoulder.

"Been a long day." He kissed the top of her head again as his hands roamed up and down her back, calming her and himself. Just touching her was enough to set his world right.

"Yes. Very long." She glanced up at him, her eyes narrow again.

"You volunteered us for this, not me."

"Yes, but you were the one who decided to run them ragged and now they're—"

"Brats?"

"Yes." She lowered her voice, glancing around as if

Maggie were standing nearby listening.

"Tell you what? Pour yourself a glass of wine and go take a shower or a nice long bath." His dick hardened at the thought of her wet and slippery, naked and waiting for him.

"Really?" Her green eyes gleamed with hope.

"Yeah." His hand drifted to her ass.

"Thank you, but I can't." Her eyes dimmed. "You're right. I agreed to this. I can't leave you to take care of them."

"I insist." He kissed her gently.

"It's not right." But she wanted to, it was all over her face.

"You can make it up to me later." One side of his mouth quirked upward in a sexy half-smile.

"You sure?" She was ready to bolt.

"Yes." It was the only way he was going to get laid tonight. Once they were alone, he wouldn't have the patience to woo her, and after a day with kids, it'd take work to get her in the mood. This would save him time in the long run and that meant he'd be fucking her that much sooner. "Now, go." He swatted her ass.

CHAPTER 18: SARAH

Sarah forced herself to walk casually to their bedroom, when she really wanted to run like the hounds from hell were after her.

"Aunt Sarah, Peter's touching me," said Isabella.

"You need to move." Peter shoved his sister. "I called the couch."

"Talk to Uncle Nick." She cringed at the look of betrayal on Nick's face as she closed the bedroom door. She leaned against it for a second but the thick piece of wood was no match for the kids' arguing. She hurried into the bathroom, grabbing her phone on the way. She turned on her music but she could still hear them. She turned up the volume and started the bath. She was the worst kind of partner, leaving him out there alone but he needed to learn that children weren't all soft kisses and giggles. Plus, the damn man had refused to listen to her. Kids needed naps or they were a nightmare.

She pulled off her clothes and turned down the water

to a trickle. Everything was quiet and then a yell from Isabella shattered the peace like a gunshot. The little girl was furious. She should go and help. She really should. She sprinkled some bath oil across the top of the water. Nick loved this scent. She'd make up abandoning him later. She got into the tub and sighed as the hot water soaked into her skin. She leaned her head back and closed her eyes. This was heaven. Quiet. Warm. Peaceful. Heaven. She reached out her hand… "Shit." She'd forgotten her wine.

She sat up, staring at the door. She could holler for Nick. Any other time, she would. He'd bring her the wine and end up in the tub with her or washing her. Her body tingled at the thought, but tonight he might dump the wine on her head. She wouldn't blame him. She leaned back against the tub. She could live without wine.

The sound of the TV drifted over her music. Poor Nick. Cartoons were okay sometimes but two nights in a row was a bit much. As soon as she was done in here, she'd tell him to go shower. He deserved some alone time too. She rested her head against the back of the tub, closing her eyes. More sounds from the TV and then arguing.

She turned off the water and stood, stepping out of the tub. She should go help him. She really should, but instead she walked to her nightstand and grabbed her ear buds. She went back to the tub. This was her time. He'd told her to go. She deserved thirty minutes and when it was over—lord help her—she'd go out there and let him have his alone time.

CHAPTER 19: NICK

Nick moaned as Sarah's mouth skimmed over his neck, kissing and nipping. This was the best dream and he didn't want to wake. Ever. He'd been having a nightmare— kids everywhere, screaming and fighting. Her tongue darted into his ear and it was like she'd licked his cock.

"Wake up, sleepyhead. Everyone's asleep." She nipped his lobe and his dick strained against his pants.

"Hmm? What?" *Everyone?* It didn't matter. She was horny and so was he. He started to shift toward her but he wasn't in bed and something weighed down his left arm.

"The kids. They're all asleep." She kissed him softly.

"Kids?" He looked down. Ah shit. It hadn't been a nightmare. The fighting kids had been real but one was missing. "Where's Peter?"

"I carried him to bed. I couldn't lift Isabella but the dogs have been out. All that's left is for you to put her to bed and then"—she slid her tongue into his ear again and he moaned, deep and guttural—"you are so getting lucky tonight."

He had to taste her. A quick kiss and then he'd take care of the kid. He turned, grabbing her chin and kissing her long and deep, his tongue probing her mouth before breaking away. He stood, making sure Isabella didn't fall headfirst onto the sofa.

"Do you want me to run you a bath?"

"No." He didn't have the patience for games or finesse. He wanted her naked with legs spread. He picked up Isabella, his gaze taking in Sarah as he straightened. She wore a T-shirt and a pair of sweats that hugged her hips. They had to go. It all had to go. "I want you"—he glanced at the sleeping child in his arms—"just like last night."

"Exactly, like last night? Toy and all?" Her cheeks heated with a soft pink tint.

"Yes. Exactly." His gaze dropped to her breasts. He wanted to tell her to lift her shirt because that rosy hue would cover her tits.

She smiled, her green eyes darkening. "Got it, but don't take too long because I might finish without you." Her eyes raked down his body, lingering like a caress on his cock.

"You'd better not fuc"—his eyes dropped to Isabella—"finish without me." He turned and strode down the hallway.

Sarah enjoyed sex as much as he did. Going without for this long had to have her on edge too. He walked into the bedroom and placed Isabella on the bed. He tossed the covers over her and headed for the door. Sarah would be undressing right now. He took a deep breath. He had to get himself under control or he'd explode when he walked into their bedroom and saw her naked and wet, waiting for him.

"Uncle Nick."

Isabella's soft tone almost made him drop to the floor and cry. Instead, he turned. "Yes."

"Where are you going?"

"To bed. Just like you." Well, not exactly. She was going to sleep the dreams of the innocent, while he was going to fuck until he passed out.

"But I'm not tired."

"Honey, you fell asleep during the show. You're tired."

"No." She sat up. "I was tired but now, I'm not."

"Please, close your eyes and go to sleep." *Please for the love of God just go to sleep.* He ran his hand through his hair, ready to tear it out. No wonder Terry was such a dick sometimes. All this frustration could turn a man into a cranky ass or a whimpering puddle. He was on the verge of both.

"But I'm not sleepy."

"You will be as soon as you close your eyes." If he didn't hurry Sarah might be done. He didn't have the fortitude to rev her back up for another orgasm until he at least had one or the way he was feeling right now about ten.

"I won't, Uncle Nick." Her eyes teared up and Nick's heart melted.

"You will." He walked back to the bed. "I promise."

"Will you read me a story?" She blinked, a large tear hanging from her long lashes. "Please."

Fuck him. Apparently girls were born with the ability to render a man helpless. "Okay. One. Only one." He prayed Sarah would wait for him. He grabbed a book from the nightstand.

"Not that one."

"What's the matter with this one? You liked it last night."

"I want a new one."

"What about this one?" He grabbed the other book.

"You read that last night too." She rolled her eyes.

"Then pick one."

"Do you have a favorite?"

"No." His favorite story was the one he and Sarah should be playing in their bedroom. "You pick."

"Any book?"

"Yes."

"Even if you don't like it?"

"Yes. Any book. Any one at all." His gaze darted to the door. Sarah had better be waiting for him.

"And you'll finish it?"

"Of course." If Sarah fell asleep, he'd…

"Promise."

"Yes. I promise. Just pick a book." He took a deep breath. "Please."

She glanced at him, a triumphant look in her eyes, as she crawled from the bed. He unconsciously leaned away from her. It was stupid. He had no reason to feel nervous.

She was a little girl but that look had made him want to run out of the room.

She rummaged through her backpack and smiled as she handed him a book. "This one."

He knew that smile. It made his stomach clench and his nuts tuck back into his body. It was the look every woman, and apparently, little girls, gave a man when she knew she'd won.

She crawled under the covers and patted the bed next to her. "Sit here, Uncle Nick."

He opened the book and almost cursed. It was a small book but it was filled with pages and pages of writing. He should've listened to his instincts and run when he'd had the chance.

CHAPTER 20: SARAH

Sarah stripped off her clothes and climbed into bed. She pulled the vibrator from her nightstand and turned it on. Her breath caught in her throat as she skimmed it over her pussy. She ran it through her wetness, making the toy slick so it slid along her folds more easily. She teased around her clit, the sensations vibrating through her and making her bite her lip. Nick had better hurry. She was used to having sex, a lot of it, and she'd been deprived for way too long. She trembled as she rubbed it harder and faster along her clit. Lord, it felt good but she forced herself to pull the toy away. She wanted an orgasm but one with Nick was always better than one without him.

She turned off the toy and dropped it next to her pillow. She stared at the door. What was taking him so long? She got up and pulled down the covers, eliminating any obstacles.

She stretched out on the bed and waited, her fingers drumming on her thigh. Her hand skimmed up her leg and over her pussy, drifting over her clit. She pulled her hand away as she glanced at the vibrator. If he didn't hurry, she was going to either use the toy or rub herself to completion. Where was he? Nick never dallied when he could be fucking. Damn man must be having trouble with the kids or he'd be in here and probably inside her already. The throb between her legs pulsed harder at the thought of him sliding deep inside her, over and over, faster and harder.

"Damn it." She rolled out of bed and pulled on her robe as she headed into the living room. The house was quiet but the light was still on in the guest room. She walked down the hallway, stopping in the doorway.

Tank and Sweetie were curled at the foot of the bed. Tank's tail flopped twice and then he closed his eyes. Sweetie looked at her, his expression both tired and happy as he placed his large head near Peter's legs.

Peter was in the bed where she'd put him still sleeping soundly. Nick was in the middle of the bed, a book resting on his chest, with Isabella curled against his side and both of them sound asleep.

She wasn't sure if she wanted to stamp her foot in frustration or melt into a puddle of mush on the floor as memories of her childhood crashed around her. She'd fallen asleep snuggled against her father many times when she'd been a kid. Her home had been happy. She'd been loved and she'd loved. Sure, there'd been struggles but overall, it'd been a good life, a great childhood. Maybe, just maybe, she could have that again but this time as the mother. Their daughter. Their son. Her heart filled with love, hope…but life was hard and unfair. Bad things happened. She knew that. She'd lived that. Sweat broke out across her skin. She'd failed her other baby. She'd fail this one too.

Isabella snuggled closer to Nick, her hand tangling in his T-shirt. Sarah liked sleeping like that too, her head on his chest listening to his strong heartbeat and knowing that she was safe, at least for the moment—no worries, no cruel fate, only a man who loved her and whom she loved.

She made her way across the room to the bed, watching them sleep. This could be hers if she were brave enough to reach for it. She leaned down and kissed Nick's forehead. "I love you and would love to have your baby but I'm terrified." A tear trailed down her cheek and she wiped it away. "What if something happens? I…I don't think I can survive losing another baby." She kissed him again and straightened. Now, she just had to find the courage to tell him this when he was awake.

CHAPTER 21: NICK

Nick woke, trying to figure out where he was. The room was dark and he was surrounded—dogs at his feet and kids on both sides. Shit. He must've fallen asleep when he'd been reading that damn book Isabella had given to him.

He gently eased out from under Isabella's arm, freezing as she mumbled something before rolling over. His heart pounded and his muscles tensed as if a tiger were stalking him instead of a couple of kids. When she snored softly, he climbed over Peter, careful not to bump him and that wasn't easy in a dark room. His feet dropped to the floor. Wait a minute. He'd been reading. The light had been on. That meant Sarah must've come by looking for him. She should've woken him. He smirked as he headed for the door. He'll make her pay for that…later. First, he needed to take the edge off his desire with a hard, fast fuck.

He closed the door behind him and strode to their bedroom, opening the door. "Why didn't…"

Sarah was sound asleep, her soft breathing calling to

him. He loved holding her while she slept—so trusting in his arms. His to protect. His to love forever. He closed the bedroom door and stripped as he made his way across the room. He crawled under the covers, pulling her to him.

His hand went under her nightgown, trailing up the smooth skin of her legs. He loved that she didn't wear underwear to bed. He'd trained her well. Now, he needed to teach her to get into bed naked. She ended up that way anyway, but he did like unwrapping his gift. His hand cupped her breast as his lips trailed up her neck to her ear. "Wake up, babe. Please. Wake up." He'd die, his dick hard and sticking straight up, if she didn't wake this time. He turned her face and kissed her, gentle at first, his lips brushing against hers and then again but this time a little harder. He skimmed his tongue across her lips, slipping inside a little, but it wasn't enough. He moaned as he kissed her harder, explored deeper. His hand cupped her pussy. "You'd better wake." He nipped her lip and she stiffened in his arms, making him stop. He almost cried in relief as her arms wrapped around him and her eyes fluttered open.

"You woke up." She blinked at him sleepily.

"I did." He kissed her softly. "But why didn't you wake me?" He rolled on top of her. He had to get inside her right now.

"I tried." She spread her legs for him, wrapping one over his hip.

"You should've tried harder and speaking of hard." He reached between them positioning his cock at her entrance.

"I did, but you wore yourself out as well as the kids."

A scream rent the air.

"No. Fuck. No." Nick froze with his dick at the door to heaven.

"Something's wrong." She pushed at his chest.

She was right. That wasn't a fight or a tantrum. That was a scream of terror. He rolled out of bed, grabbing his pants and pulling them on as Sarah yanked on her housecoat and they both ran out of the room and down the hallway.

"The door's shut," she said.

"I shut it." He opened the door and turned on the light.

Isabella and Peter were clinging to each other and crying as Tank and Sweetie licked their wet faces.

"What's wrong?" He hurried into the room.

"I'm scared," sobbed Peter.

"Me too," said Isabella.

Davy fussed in the crib and Sarah went to him. "He's wet." She grabbed another pull-up diaper from the bag and put the baby on the floor. He chatted and made other baby noises as she changed him.

Nick turned back to the two crying kids. "What's wrong? Why are you scared?"

"There's a monster in here," said Peter. "A zombie."

Nick's jaw clenched at Sarah's huff. "There's no such thing as a zombie."

"Yes, there is," said Isabella.

"No, there's not. It's just pretend."

Sarah stood, grabbing the baby and heading for the door.

"Where are you going?

"He's hungry."

"Okay. Feed him and then we'll…" His eyes darted down her body.

"Oh, that's not going to happen tonight."

"Why not?" There was no way he was going another night without fucking.

She nodded at Isabella and Peter.

"They'll be fine." He turned to the kids. "Won't you? There's no reason to be scared. Plus"—he patted the dogs—"these two wouldn't let anyone or anything get you."

"Really?" asked Isabella.

"Yes." He flicked his fingers toward the door, sending Sarah on her way. She needed to feed the baby, get him to sleep and then get her cute little ass back in their bed.

"I don't know." Isabella frowned at the dogs. "They might get scared and run away."

"Nah." Peter was easier to convince than his sister. He patted Tank. "He'd protect me from zombies?"

"Yep." Nick scratched the dog's ear. "He's a former marine. Monsters don't scare him."

"They don't?" Peter stared at him wide eyed.

"Nope. How about I read you a story to get your mind off monsters?" He grabbed some books from the kids' backpacks.

"Okay." Peter dropped onto his back, pulling the covers up to his chin.

Isabella stared at him, frowning. "You turned off the

light."

"Ah…" He wasn't going to tattle on Sarah. "I won't do it again. I promise."

He stretched out between them and began to read. He'd finished his third book before Sarah came back into the room with Davy.

She cradled the baby in her arms, his chubby cheek pressed against the top of her breast. Nick's heart melted at the thought of her carrying their baby like this—her breasts larger, full of milk. She kissed Davy's head before gently placing him in the crib and covering him.

"Good night." She bent and kissed Isabella on the forehead. "There's nothing to be scared of here." Her eyes darted to Nick.

For the first time since the kids had arrived, he didn't see a hint of fear in hers. Maybe she was exhausted or so horny she couldn't think of anything but him. He snorted. Not likely. That was more his style than hers.

She moved to the other side of the bed, her hand trailing over Sweetie and then Tank before she bent and kissed Peter who was almost asleep. "Sweet dreams. Your mommy and Daddy Terry will be here tomorrow."

The sooner that happened the better, but Nick kept that thought to himself. Sarah glanced at him as she left. Her face serene and unreadable. He didn't like that. He'd thought he could read her perfectly. He hurried and finished the book.

"Another one," said Isabella.

He wanted to refuse but he recognized that stubborn

tilt to her lips, another trait females seemed to be born with. "One more and then you go to sleep."

"Okay." She handed him her dictionary of mermaids and other crap.

"No. Not this one."

"You promised."

Lucky for him, he was an expert on women. It was time to lie. "I already finished it. It's not my fault you fell asleep."

Her eyes narrowed but she grabbed another book. By the time he was done reading it, her eyes were drifting shut. He climbed out of the bed.

"Night, Uncle Nick," she whispered.

"Night." He started to close the door.

"Leave it open. Please." Panic laced her soft tone.

"Okay but just this once."

She relaxed back onto the pillow and he hurried down the hallway, his dick rising. He threw open the bedroom door and almost cheered.

"Are they asleep?" Sarah was awake, leaning against the headboard, the sheet pulled up to her chest.

"Yep. Drop the covers." He pushed his pants down as she let go of the sheet and shifted, so it fell. "Fuck, you're gorgeous." His mouth was dry but he knew where to find an abundance of wetness to quench his parched throat. "Kick the covers off and spread your legs." His voice was raspy and raw with desire. The old Nick would be embarrassed at how much he needed her but the new Nick, Sarah's Nick, was glad she knew that he was risking as much as she was.

She flung the covers aside and opened her legs. His nostrils flared at the sight of her damp curls. She reached between her thighs, opening her folds for him. He didn't remember moving but the next thing he knew he was on the bed, kissing her as his fingers joined hers between her legs.

She moaned under him and he shoved two fingers inside her. She was so hot and wet, so ready for him. "Now, Sarah. Now."

"No."

He teased his cock along her slick folds. His eyes closing at the pleasure.

"Nick. Stop."

It took a moment for him to realize that she was no longer pulling him closer but instead pushing him away.

"What?" There was a soft tap on their door. "No." He wanted to weep. To scream. To shove inside her and ignore the sound. "It can't be."

"Get off me." She pushed at him.

"Wait. Not yet." He'd waited forever to get back here. He wasn't giving in yet. His chest heaved as he said, "What do you want?"

"Nick. They're kids." She slapped his chest.

"They're annoying." And they were going to make him a eunuch if they didn't stop interrupting him.

"I'm scared," came a soft voice through the doorway.

"Shit-fuck." He rolled to the side, his cock deflating like an old balloon.

"Cover up." She crawled from the bed.

"Why? There's nothing for them to see except a dying man who'll never have a boner again."

"This isn't exactly fun for me either."

"You agreed to this." He sat up, yanking the covers over himself.

"Because you wouldn't stop talking about having kids." She pulled on her robe.

"That's bullshit. I may have mentioned it a few times."

"A few? How about every day at least once a day." She walked to the door.

"Maybe I wouldn't have mentioned it so much if you'd talked to me about it instead of freaking out."

"I did not freak out. I barely said a word." She glared at him as she opened the door.

"And that's so much better." He punched his pillow because he had nothing else to punch.

Both Peter and Isabella stood in the doorway, their hands clasped together. Tank and Sweetie trotted into the room and curled up on their beds.

"What's the matter?" She bent, brushing a tear from Peter's face.

"We're scared," repeated Isabella.

"Zombies," said Peter.

Nick almost snarled at her I-told-you-so look. It'd been a good idea. Perhaps he hadn't deployed it correctly, but who runs from unicorns or kittens.

"There's no reason to be scared," she said.

"Can we sleep with you?" Peter looked longingly at the bed.

"You've got to be fu…" He shook his head. "Why not? Nothing else is going to happen in here besides sleeping."

Peter and Isabella started toward the bed when Sarah grabbed them. "First, let's get a drink of water and then go to the bathroom."

"I'm not thirsty," said Isabella.

"I don't have to go potty," said Peter.

"Well, we're going to do it anyway." She ushered them out the door, glancing over her shoulder at him. "Don't just lie there. Get dressed."

"I don't wear—"

"Pajamas." She sent him a speaking look and nodded at the kids. "And you don't have to tonight. Sweats and a T-shirt are fine. Like always."

"Right. Like always." Like never. He hadn't worn anything to bed since Sarah had come home from the clinic.

CHAPTER 22: NICK

Nick put the last of the brunch dishes away as Sarah wiped Davy's face.

"Can we watch TV?" asked Isabella.

"Yeah, go ahead." The two older kids bolted out of the kitchen as he turned on the dishwasher and leaned against the counter, checking his watch. "Terry and Maggie will be here soon." *They'd better be.*

"We made it." She smiled softly at him and kissed Davy's chubby cheek as the baby squirmed in her arms.

Nick's belly filled with heat but although there was desire in the warmth it wasn't lust, but love, hope and scary wonderful feelings. She no longer looked at the baby as if the kid would turn into a kraken and devour her. "I think we did good."

"I don't know if I'd go that far. We did okay, but good is a stretch." She put the baby down and he toddled into the living room after his brother and sister.

"We did great." He grabbed her hand and pulled her

into his arms.

"I don't think great babysitters scare the kids so badly that they have to sleep with them."

"Okay. Lesson learned." His hands cupped her ass. "But the kids are alive and"—he kissed her softly—"how do you do it?"

"Do what?"

"I love you. You know that. I know that." He ignored the tightening of her body. "I can't imagine loving you more than I do but every day I'm around you that's exactly what happens." She almost melted into him and he kissed her, his tongue teasing across her lips. "I love you, Sarah Daly. Even though my heart is full, somehow, you make it grow and I love you even more." He smiled wickedly at her. "One day it's going to be as big as you make my dick."

"You sure know how to ruin the romance." She laughed, slapping his chest.

"What? That's romantic."

"The first part, yes."

He frowned, fighting his smile. "The second part's romantic too. This"—he pulled her into his growing erection—"is a huge part of romance."

"No." She wiggled against him. "That's lust and sex and they are wonderful but it isn't romance."

"But it is. Fucking you is the most romantic thing I can do."

She laughed. "Let me give you a lesson in romance. If you say dick or fuck, it isn't romantic."

"No." He feigned shock. "You don't mean that."

"I do."

"I'll get you to admit that you're wrong."

"Never." But her eyes heated to a warm green.

"We'll see about that as soon as the kids le…"

The doorbell rang. Tank and Sweetie barked, running to the door.

"They're here." He shoved her aside as he raced to the door. "Kids, your mom's here."

CHAPTER 23: SARAH

Sarah cringed as the noise level in the house rose to a crescendo of barks, screams of excitement and children talking—loudly—at once.

Maggie smiled as she walked over to Sarah. "We brought lunch." She held up two large bags. "A small thank you."

"Oh. You're welcome. It was…fun but we just finished breakfast."

"Just finished breakfast?" Terry strolled into the kitchen—Davy in his arms, Peter clinging to his back and Isabella holding his hand. "How late did you let the kids stay up?"

"They were in bed early," Nick almost snapped. "But they couldn't sleep."

"Were they sick?" Maggie glanced over her shoulder as she began pulling the food from the bags and placing it on the counter.

"We were scared of zombies," said Peter.

"You let them watch horror movies?" Terry sounded appalled.

"No. We're not stupid." Nick came to Sarah's side, taking her hand.

"At least one of us isn't," she mumbled. Nick shot her a glare. She'd feel bad except these guys told each other everything anyway.

"What was that?" Terry pulled Peter from his back and sat on a chair, putting both boys on his lap. "I smell a story."

"There's no story." Nick's jaw was tense.

"Peter, what made you think of zombies?" Terry sent him a smug look.

Sarah clamped her hand tighter on Nick's as he almost growled.

"I don't know," said Peter.

Nick smirked.

"I wasn't scared when we were being chased by the zombie at the park," said Peter.

"You were too," said Isabella. "Uncle Nick had to stop pretending all the time so you didn't cry."

Sarah bit her lip as Nick's smirk slid from his face.

"Tattletale," he muttered to Isabella.

"There are no secrets with children," said Terry.

"Kids, are you hungry?" Maggie held a paper plate, ready to fill it. "We have a long drive."

"Mommy, Uncle Nick taught me to dive. Can I show you?" Isabella almost vibrated with excitement.

"Ah…" Maggie glanced at Terry.

"Maybe some other time," said Nick. "You guys have a long drive and probably should get going."

"Nonsense." Terry's dark eyes sparkled with mischief. "We have plenty of time." He put the two boys down. "Go get your swimsuits on and bring Davy's here."

"Yeah!" The two kids ran from the room, Davy hurrying after them.

"Terry," Maggie's eyes darted to Sarah. "I think they might want to be alone after a weekend with kids."

"Nah. They're fine." Terry smirked.

"Leave, asshole," said Nick.

"Nick." She slapped his arm.

"No, it's all right." Maggie laughed. "Kids can be a handful even when you're used to them, let alone having three dumped on you."

"They were wonderful and we had a great time." It was mostly true. As difficult as it had been, she was going to miss having the little ones around.

"Thank you for saying that but I'm sure there were times…" Maggie grinned. "Sometimes I want to string them up and I'm their mother."

"No. Really. It was fun." *Mostly*.

"Since the kids aren't hungry, we should get going." Maggie tossed the burgers back in the bag.

"They want to show us how Uncle Nick taught them to dive." Terry shot Nick a smug look.

"They can show us at the hotel," said Maggie.

"Please, stay for a bit. Watch the kids and then eat before you head out." It was the polite thing to say. Plus, her friend looked happy, really, really happy and Sarah wanted to hear how the weekend had gone.

"What the hell?" Nick stared at her like she was a traitor.

Terry laughed but Maggie's face fell a bit.

"Nick, stop it. You're being rude."

"Being backed up does that to a man, especially, Nick," said Terry. "He's being downright angelic compared to when he was celibate for four months."

"Shut the fu…shut up," said Nick.

"I, on the other hand, can control my temper even when my baser needs have gone…unfulfilled," said Terry.

"Bullshit. You're only saying that because you just spent a weekend fu"—Nick glanced at the door—"at the Club."

"It was lovely." Maggie walked over and took Terry's hand. "Thank you both for watching the kids."

Terry looked up at her, adoration and heat in his dark gaze, and raised her hand to his lips, kissing her knuckles. Maggie stared down at him with such love that Sarah's heart turned to mush. There was something different about the couple and it was good different.

"Maggie's right." Terry kissed her hand again. "Since you did us a favor, we should get going."

Isabella burst into the room. "Here's Davy's suit. Let's go to the pool."

"Nope. Can't." Terry stood. "We need to leave."

"But you said." Isabella's eyes widened with hurt.

"Sorry, but Uncle Nick wants—"

"To take you to the pool. Give me a minute to put on my suit." Nick turned to Terry, lowering his voice. "That was low even for you."

Terry shrugged. "I won. It's all that matters."

"Terry." Maggie shook her head as she grabbed Davy's swimsuit and began tugging off the baby's clothes.

CHAPTER 24: NICK

Nick got out of the pool as the women ushered the kids inside to change.

Terry walked over and handed him a scotch. "Here."

"Thanks." He sat on one of the lounge chairs and took a long sip. "You not drinking?" He glanced at the iced tea in Terry's hand.

"Nah. Got a long drive."

Nick nodded and took another drink. "I did enjoy the kids."

"Children are great." Terry stretched out on another chair.

"Yeah."

"But…" Terry studied him.

"I think Sarah was right. I'm not ready to have children. I like our life as it is."

"Understandable. Kids turn your life inside out and they always come first." Terry sat up, leaning forward with elbows on his knees. "When you do decide to have them, take some advice from me. Make time for the two of you."

He stared into his glass. "I didn't with my ex-wife and maybe if I had…" He cleared his throat. "I wouldn't change anything, not now. I...the way I feel about Maggie…"

"Admit it. You love her."

Terry shrugged.

Nick almost choked on his drink as he pointed at his friend. "That's an admission."

"It was a shrug."

"You didn't deny it."

"How I feel about Maggie is none of your business."

"You don't have to say it. It's written all over that frowning face of yours." Nick grinned, shaking his head. "The man who'd sworn he'd never love again and said love was for fools and—"

"I was wrong."

"What?" Nick gasped. "No. Did the world end." He looked around.

"Stop being an ass."

"Seriously. Where's my phone? I need to record this for future generations. Terry, the arrogant ass, who thinks he's always right just admitted that he was wrong."

"Shut the fuck up. I never said I was always right."

"Oh, you've said that. Hundreds...thousands of times."

"Well"—Terry took a sip of his drink and then smiled—"this is the exception that makes the rule."

Nick snorted. "I have no idea how Maggie puts up with you."

"Me either, but she does and I intend to keep it that

way." Terry stared over Nick's shoulder at the pool for a long moment. "Don't let anything mess up what you and Sarah have."

"I don't plan on it." He'd do everything he could to make sure that didn't happen.

"I'm serious about making time for each other. It'll be tough when you do have kids but find a way. It might save your marriage."

He'd never seen Terry so serious. Love was a scary-assed thing. Sometimes, he was still terrified at how much he needed Sarah. "I doubt it would've saved yours. Your ex liked women. It's not your fault it took her years to admit it to herself."

"I know but I'm still not making the same mistake with Maggie."

"Soundproofing your master bedroom should do the trick." It was a frigging brilliant idea that he had no qualms about stealing. "If you're happy with the work, give me the guy's name."

"Will do. Get that done before the kids arrive. Then your sex life won't have to suffer…as much."

"Sex life? After kids? That's not possible." Nick tossed back his drink. This weekend had taught him that he couldn't have both a great sex life and children. So for now, the choice was easy—sex. "It's a wonder people ever have more than one."

"Parents find a way." Terry laughed. "You have to be creative and spontaneous."

"Trust me, that wasn't the problem. The kids wouldn't

sleep and then if we got the two to sleep Davy woke. And if that wasn't enough, they were scared of the dark and everything else." He tipped back his empty glass searching for the last drop.

"Yeah, sometimes it's like that."

"Sometimes? Not always?" Maybe they could have some kids.

"Get the kids on a routine from the start. They sleep better. This weekend was not normal—new house, new dogs." Terry waved his hand. "They were bound to sleep poorly."

"Makes sense but…How do you do it? I know you. You like sex—a lot—and I…I don't see how you manage. The kids are great and I'm sure it's worth it." He wasn't, not at all. Having sex only at night and if they weren't too exhausted didn't sound like a life he wanted.

Terry studied him.

"Okay. I'm a selfish jerk but I don't think children are in my future. Maybe I'll change my mind later but shit, I haven't gotten laid since your kids got here. That's all weekend. I don't want to live like that." There he'd said it out loud. He was an asshole but it was the truth.

"You don't have to go without."

"I know, but only at night? A quickie before the kids wake…" He frowned, shaking his head.

"That's not what I'm talking about." Terry leaned forward, glancing at the door to the house. "You can't tell anyone."

"I tell Sarah everything."

"Then forget it." Terry leaned back against the seat. "Come to me after you have kids and if you ask really nicely, I might tell you how to manage to have sex—a lot of sex—with kids around."

"You're lying." His friend had to be. It wasn't possible.

"Am I?" Terry's eyebrow raised. "Do you really think I'm okay with just having a nighttime fumble in the dark?"

"No." That wasn't Terry's style any more than it was his.

"Trust me. You need to know this but you won't want her to know." Terry's eyes darted to the door. "It's the one thing I don't share with Maggie."

"You don't?" He didn't like keeping secrets from Sarah.

"Nope. She'd want me to stop." Terry smirked. "Not that I would but then we'd fight and..." He shook his head. "Here's another lesson. Avoid the fight whenever you can."

"Duh."

"Sounds easy but it's not. Like this. If I told her, we'd end up fighting. If she ever finds out, we'll end up fighting even more because I kept it from her. So, it's in my best interest not to tell anyone."

"But you're going to tell me." He needed to know. Terry was never this closed-mouthed about anything. The man was brutally honest.

"I was because I felt I owed you. I wouldn't have had this weekend if it weren't for you and Sarah." Terry's lips curled in a smirk. "But I'm off the hook. I offered to tell you but you refused. Your choice. Debt paid."

"Debt paid? No way. You still owe me."

"Nope. I offered payment and you refused. We're even."

"I haven't had sex in over two days. You owe me."

"That's your problem and when you have kids it'll be your life."

"Fine. I won't tell Sarah." He didn't like it but he'd do it. He had to know the secret. Terry would never go two days without sex.

"No. I'm not telling you now. The opportunity has passed."

"I'll tell Maggie you're keeping something from her." He wasn't a novice at negotiations.

"Now, who's the ass?"

"I learn from the best."

"That's true." Terry tipped his glass in salute and then finished his tea. "Swear you won't tell Sarah because she'll tell Maggie."

"I swear."

"I don't trust you."

"Come on." He didn't like how desperate he sounded, but hell, he was desperate.

"Okay but"—Terry's eyes met his—"if you tell Sarah, you give up your membership to the Club."

"That's not—"

"That's the only way I'm telling you."

"Fine." He didn't like it but Sarah couldn't get mad if she didn't know.

"I bribe Isabella."

"You do what?"

"I pay Isabella to watch her brothers. The longer they all get along and are quiet the more money she gets."

"And Maggie's okay with this?"

"No. I told you. She doesn't know."

"Oh. Right." His friend had said that.

"You'll have to wait for your second kid to use this tactic but it's easy to find time for sex around the first kid. When the baby sleeps you can fuck however you want."

"So, you give her money and you and Maggie—"

"Yep." Terry couldn't look smugger if he tried.

"Doesn't Maggie get suspicious?"

"Nope. She puts them in front of the TV with drinks and snacks." He grinned. "She thinks it's her food and the television that's keeping them quiet." His smile slipped a bit. "I was concerned the first few times. Before I started bribing Isabella, we'd no sooner get in the room and naked before the kids started fighting."

"I understand that." He cringed as memories of the weekend of frustration flooded his head.

Terry nodded, a frown on his handsome face. "I thought my balls were going to be Smurf blue."

"I wondered the same thing about mine." Nick glanced at his crotch. They'd been the normal color today but a lifetime of interruptions would taint them at the very least.

"Maggie was suspicious at first, especially after Peter and Davy started fighting but Isabella calmed them down. Then she decided that it must be the new vitamins that the kids were taking." He laughed. "They're fucking multivitamins but she believes they're the reason the kids aren't fighting when we're alone." He shook his head. "She'd be appalled that it's the multivitamin of the world— cash. Cold, hard, cash that was and is the great motivator. I'm just lucky that Isabella is fiendishly drawn to it."

"You could've mentioned this to me. I would've paid her a fortune for one hour. Thirty minutes. Fuck, five minutes."

"This weekend was a surprise for me."

"Yeah, but once you knew you could've texted me."

"I wasn't exactly thinking of you and your sex life when Maggie told me we'd be spending the weekend at the Club."

"I suppose not."

"On down times, I did wonder how you were faring."

"Then why the hell didn't you text?"

"Because Maggie told me that Sarah wanted to use this weekend to make you realize that you weren't ready for a baby." Terry stood. "I figured I'd let you handle it on your own. You learned a lesson you'll never forget."

"Asshole." He'd thought it before but this confirmed it. He needed new friends.

"Yep, but now you know the secret to having kids and having sex." He headed for the door. "Oh, and definitely get your room soundproofed." He paused. "And locks. Get lots of locks. For your bedroom. Bathroom. Garage. Actually, put one on every door. And don't forget your toy cabinet. You don't want to scar your kids when they realize that Daddy likes to whip Mommy and Mommy likes to be punished."

CHAPTER 25: SARAH

Sarah sat on the couch next to Maggie. Davy was playing on the floor and the two bigger kids were showering.

"I really can't thank you enough for watching them." Maggie took a sip of her iced tea.

"I enjoyed it." *Mostly.*

"I'm glad. I know you wanted to teach Nick a lesson but when you two do decide to have kids of your own, you'll make a good mother."

"Thank you." No, she wouldn't. Cold fear flooded her veins. She'd had her chance. She'd had a baby inside her and she...hadn't wanted it.

"I mean it, Sarah." Maggie leaned forward and squeezed her hand. "I know it's scary but you'll be a wonderful mother and Nick"—she smiled—"he'll be a great father. He's kind of a big kid himself."

Sarah laughed, thinking of Nick always pushed her fear aside. "That's the truth, but he's responsible too. He did a lot with them."

"Oh, I didn't mean anything bad by that."

"I know."

Maggie face softened as she glanced through the window at Terry. "Who would've thought that men like them could be so great around kids."

"Not me." Sarah felt her own face soften when she looked at Nick. She loved that man more than was safe.

"I thought Terry was an egotistical, selfish, arrogant ass when I first met him."

"You weren't wrong." Sarah smiled to take the sting from her words.

Maggie laughed. "No, but he's so much more than that."

"I know and he seems…happy. Happier than before this weekend." She hesitated, prying wasn't polite but Annie would kill her if she didn't at least try and find out what had happened to make Terry and Maggie so sickeningly happy. "So, you had a good time?"

"We did."

"I'm glad." That wasn't much to go on. Her mind spun. "I was a little concerned. The Club can be…surprising the first time you visit. I know it was for me."

"It wasn't completely new to me. I had been there twice before."

"Those times don't count." Her friend was being deliberately obtuse. She should stop digging for dirt but she really, really wanted to know what had happened.

"Why not?"

"Because the first time you were there by accident and the second time you and Terry left instead of staying and playing." She leaned forward, her voice lowering. "It's completely different when you're there to play."

"That's true." Maggie's eyes grew distant. "It was beyond anything I'd ever imagined and my imagination has improved a lot since I met Terry."

Sarah laughed. "I bet it has. These guys do know their way around a woman's body and an adult toy shop."

"It was more than that." Maggie glanced down at her hand.

Sarah held her breath. The showers had stopped. The kids would be out here soon but Maggie didn't say anything. She couldn't wait any longer. "What happened? Both of you looked relaxed beyond the point of breathing and that I get. Great sex and multiple orgasms can do that, but something else is going on."

"Sarah." Maggie's eyes widened. "I expected prying from Annie but not you."

"Sorry, but I'm dying to know what happened. Both of you look...I can't explain it. Beyond happy."

"He said—"

"Mom, I need my clothes." Isabella stood in the doorway to the master bedroom.

Sarah bit her lip to stop from shouting "no". This was almost as bad as being interrupted during sex.

"I told you to take them when you went to shower." Maggie stood and headed for the guest bedroom.

"I forgot. Sorry."

"It's okay." Maggie came back out and handed her daughter a backpack. "Now, hurry up and get dressed."

As soon as Isabella closed the door, Sarah patted the couch. "Sit. Tell me. What did he say?"

"He said—"

"What did I say?" Terry strode into the house.

"Why do you assume *he* means you?" asked Nick as he closed the sliding glass door behind him.

"Maggie was talking. It was about me." Terry shrugged.

"Please. She could've been talking about Davy or Peter or any other male. Maybe even me," said Nick.

Terry shot him a disgusted look before turning toward Maggie. "Who were you talking about?"

"Ah..."

"The truth, rabbit, or..."

Davy toddled over to him. "Up."

Terry bent, lifting the baby.

"We were talking about you." Maggie seemed to force it out.

"See." Terry sent Nick a smug expression.

"You couldn't have lied?" Nick shook his head. "Anyone else want a drink?" He headed for the kitchen.

"No, thank you," said Maggie.

"I'll take one," said Sarah. Iced tea was nice but a glass of wine would be lovely.

"We need to get going," said Terry.

Nick stopped in the doorway, his eyes darting to his friend. "Don't fuck with me."

"Nick." Sarah almost choked.

Maggie laughed. "Nonsense." She leaned over and hugged Sarah, whispering, "I feel the same way when David is late to get the kids. I love them to death but I love my alone time with Terry too."

"And your kids were rough on poor Nick," said Terry.

"Oh, dear." Maggie cringed. "That bad."

"Peter's marksmanship was spot on," said Terry.

"I'm so sorry. I have no idea how he can always hit a man right there." Maggie's hand fluttered in front of her abdomen.

"He should teach a self-defense course," muttered Nick.

"The streets would be much safer." Terry laughed.

"Can we go in the pool at the hotel?" Isabelle ran out of the room, her backpack, dragging behind her.

"You're going to turn into a fish," said Terry.

"Maybe if you're good in the car," said Maggie.

"We'll be good." Peter came out of the guest bedroom.

"Don't forget your backpack," said Sarah.

"Oh, right." He ran back into the room and returned a minute later, backpack strapped over his shoulders.

"I should make sure they didn't leave anything." Sarah stood and headed for the bedroom.

"You're acting like a mother already." Maggie smiled at her.

Her friend was right and it was both terrifying and exciting.

CHAPTER 26: SARAH

Sarah closed the door as Terry and Maggie's car backed out of their driveway. She braced herself for Nick's attack. The man was used to sex at least three times a day. They had some catching up to do. Her body melted at the thought, but he moved to the window and peeked out the curtains.

"Uhm…What are you doing?" She walked over to him, resting her hand on his back. She was used to sex three times a day too.

"Watching them leave."

"Why?" Her hand trailed down to his ass and gave it a little squeeze. She wanted to nibble her way across the firm mounds.

"Because, if I get interrupted one more time when I'm fucking you, I am literally going to curl into a ball and cry."

"I'm pretty sure you already did that this weekend."

"Doesn't mean I won't do it again." He smiled as he turned, pulling her flush against him. "I didn't think you'd noticed that."

"I wanted to cry too." She wrapped her arms around his neck. "Don't ever pull out like that again." Her entire body had revolted at the betrayal.

"Got it." He unbuttoned her pants. "Next time, we let the baby cry." He shoved them down her hips and she kicked them aside. "I hear it's good for them to cry a bit."

"I've heard that too." She slipped her hands inside his swim trunks and caressed his cock. "It's probably good for you as well."

"Nope." He cupped her pussy, a long finger slipping underneath the side of her underwear. "Crying only works for babies. Trust me, when men cry, they don't get what they want. If they did, men would be sobbing for pussy all the time."

His lips came down on hers and she opened for him, moaning as his tongue invaded her mouth and his fingers played in her folds. She needed him inside her now. He seemed to agree because he turned, pushing her against the window.

"Nick," she panted as he slipped a finger inside, stroking her. "Anyone can see me. We have to move." She wanted him, but they had neighbors.

He sidestepped as he shoved her shirt up, her bra down and captured her nipple with his mouth.

She tangled her fingers in his thick, soft hair and pulled him closer as his teeth and tongue sent sparks of pleasure shooting through her body. She rocked against his hand, but she needed more. She needed him. "Please, Nick. Stop playing and…" She gasped as he bit down on her nipple and shoved three fingers inside her. "Again. Do that again." She'd crawl up the man's arm if she were able. That'd felt so fucking good.

"I thought you wanted me to stop playing." He curled his fingers, hitting that spot and her body tensed.

"Stop." She was going to break apart. She'd been on edge for days.

"That's not your Safeword."

"I'm going to come."

"That's the plan." He stroked harder and faster, his fingers rubbing against her g-spot over and over.

"Oh…I want…you…inside…" It didn't matter what she wanted. Her body was in control and it demanded release. She bucked against his hand as he stroked her over the edge. She groaned as he pulled his hand from between her legs, her pussy still clenching, still searching for that pleasure. "Please." She was so empty and then he pushed inside her, his cock long and hard. She screamed, trembling, as her pussy tried to squeeze his cock and make room for it at the same time. It was pleasure and pain, intense and inseparable.

"That's it." He cupped her cheeks in his large hands. "Breathe, baby. Deep breaths."

She stared into his dark eyes, following his orders, giving him control, and her body relaxed around his cock. As soon as she did, he pumped into her in short, hard jabs. She was still half-coming and it only took a moment before she clamped onto his shoulders. "Nick. I'm…I'm so close.

Again." She'd had multiples with him numerous times but this was different. This hadn't ended before the next wave crashed over her.

"Good." He lifted her, placing her arms over her head as his dick and body pinned her to the wall. There was nothing holding her but him—his hands, his dick—and that slide in and out, over and over. Her legs tightened around him, trying to get some grounding.

"Oh no, you don't." He joined her hands, clasping them in one of his and yanking her legs from his waist.

"Nick, please." She dangled in the air, bumping against the wall with each of his thrusts.

"Just me, Sarah. Nothing but me." His hips rocked and his chest heaved against hers, making her nipples ache with each brush.

She was weightless, nothing but a mass of sensations. His chest hair, rubbing against her sensitive nipples. His dick, long and hot and hard, sliding into her faster and faster. His breath caressing her cheek while his eyes, dark and hot, pierced her soul.

She was him. He was her. They were one in the most elemental way. He captured her lips as his movements became faster and harder, her legs lifted but he slapped her thigh.

"I've got you. Trust me."

His words slipped into her mouth and were absorbed by her soul. She let everything go. It was only him. His body. His commands. His motion. She fell into his eyes and sparks ignited where they touched, spread where they were joined. She spiraled upward, her breath coming faster and faster, her nipples rubbing harder against his chest.

"Fuck. Sarah." He let go of her hands, his thrusts almost violent in their speed and strength and it made her shake and quiver.

She clutched his shoulders, her fingernails digging into his skin, driving him to fuck her harder. He reached between them, pressing down on her clit and her body bucked, her mouth opening in a silent scream as she shattered.

CHAPTER 27: NICK

Nick rested his forehead against Sarah's. He still had her pinned to the wall, his dick buried deep inside her and he had no intentions of leaving anytime soon. He grabbed her ass and stepped away from the wall.

She curled around him, her legs surrounding his hips and her arms around his neck as he carried her to their bedroom. He climbed onto the bed, trying really hard not to dislodge his penis. He dropped to his back with her draped across his chest.

"Where do you think you're going?" He grabbed her ass, stopping her from rolling to the side.

"Nowhere." She kissed him. "I promise." She shifted again and he tightened his grip.

"Seems to me that you're trying to go somewhere."

"Just to the side so I don't squish you."

"You're fine right where you are."

"I'm too heavy."

"Nope." His fingers trailed up and down her back,

loving the smooth, soft texture of her skin. She was soft everywhere and yet she was the strongest person he knew.

"Nick. This can't be comfortable for you."

"My dick's inside you. Where it's been trying to get all weekend. You owe me some time in there."

"Owe you?" She laughed but relaxed against him. "It's not a bed and breakfast you know."

"Should be." He kissed the top of her head. "It's warm, comfortable and I love to come here. Pun intended."

"That you do." She laughed again, her hand trailing along his chest.

"I think I'll stay here. Move in."

"Going to make work tough."

"Nah. That's what computers are for."

"What about going to the bathroom?"

"Okay. I'll leave for that, but all other deposits I'm going to make right here." He rocked his hips, loving how her body instinctively tightened around him.

"Brunch at your parent's house is going to be interesting."

He laughed. "Mom will be fine with it. She wants more grandkids." His smile slipped away and his eyes grew serious. "About that."

"Yes." She tensed immediately and this time he let her roll off him.

He turned to his side so he could see her. "You were right. I...I don't think I want kids, yet."

Her chest almost collapsed in relief.

"I like our life." He brushed some of her hair away

from her face.

"Me too." She kissed him. It was soft and sweet—a satiated lover's kiss.

"But I do want them sometime in the future." He fought not to wrap her in his arms and wash away the fear and uncertainty from her green eyes.

Her lips tightened with tension and then a fake smile spread across her face. "I guess that means, I won the bet."

"Sarah." He wanted to finish this conversation. Fix all her problems but according to Dr. Smileworth that wasn't how it worked.

"I get whatever I want." She rolled to her back. "Hmm. I've never done pegging."

"And you never will." He leaned over her. His instincts told him to chase her down, force her to talk about her fears but the doctor had said that was the last thing he should do.

"You said anything." Her eyes sparkled in challenge but behind that was insecurity.

"And I meant it but you'd never ask me to do anything that I really didn't want to do. Just like I wouldn't ask you."

"You're taking the fun away from my victory."

"Sorry." He smiled, but it was fake like hers. "Go for it. Tease me about pegging and getting fucked in the ass by some guy while you watch."

"Why bother?" Her fingers caressed his cheek. "Teasing is no fun, now that the secret is out in the open."

"Secret?"

"That I'd never ask you to do anything like that. Anything I know you really don't want to do."

Fuck, he loved this woman more than anything. "If I thought you really wanted to do it, I'd give it a try."

"You'd let me put a dildo in your butt?" Her eyes almost popped from her head.

His spine stiffened and his teeth almost ground to powder but he forced himself to nod. He cleared the disgust from his throat. "If you really, really wanted to try. Yes. I don't know. Maybe. Do you want to do that?"

"No. I don't." Her face softened and she kissed him. "I have no interest in putting anything in your ass although I've heard that you might enjoy milking."

"Perhaps." He kissed her, letting his tongue dip into her mouth for a quick taste. "If you want to put your finger in my ass, I guess we could try it." He kissed her again, his dick starting to rise with the conversation. "Some guys enjoy it."

"Do you want to try it?"

"No. Not really."

"Me either." She ran her finger over his lip and he nipped it.

"What do you want?" He knew what he wanted—her with his ring on her finger.

"I want to be in control."

"We do that."

"Without you cheating."

"I don't ch—"

"You do. You always take off the handcuffs or the restraints."

"Not my fault you don't tie them right." She slapped

155

his chest and he grabbed her hands, pinning them to her sides. "And you never complain during. As a matter of fact, I think you like it better not knowing when I'll take the control from you and fuck your brains out."

"Well…" She smiled. "There is that."

He captured her face and kissed her again, this one darker and deeper. He was hard and ready. He'd been denied too long but she pulled away, slipping out from under him. Apparently they weren't done talking. He flopped onto his back, watching her.

"I…I have to tell you something." Her smile faltered.

"Okay." He took her hand. "Anything. You can tell me anything. You know that."

"I know." The fake smile reappeared. "But I'm afraid it'll take away from my win."

His jaw tensed but he nodded. "You'll have to take the chance." He prayed she'd take a chance on them, on him. One day, she'd trust him completely. It might not be until they were eighty but he loved her enough to give her whatever time she needed.

CHAPTER 28: SARAH

Sarah was a coward. She loved Nick. He loved her. Why was she always so scared?

"I promise that no matter what you tell me, I'll give you one night of you being in control—complete control."

That wasn't the real problem and by the tension in his jaw and the disappointment in his eyes, he knew that. She had to fess up. She'd start small. Baby steps as Dr. Smileworth said.

"You were right too. I…I did enjoy the kids and I do want children. Later. Not now." Her heart raced at the terror of finding herself pregnant again.

"I'm glad." His fingers intertwined with hers. "One day. Maybe a few years after we marry." He tugged and she stretched out by his side.

"Yeah." She kissed his chest. They could talk later. "I guess that means you won too."

"I guess it does." His hand trailed up her back, sending tingles of banked passion swirling through her body.

"What do you want?" Her hand skimmed across his abdomen, her nails lightly caressing. "You can have anything." She leaned up and licked his nipple. "Anything at all. Even anal."

His eyes shot to hers. "You don't have to agree to that because I agreed to"—he shivered—"pegging."

"I know that." She kissed his chest again. "I've been thinking about anal and—"

"You have?"

"Yeah." Annie liked it so it couldn't be too bad. "I think, I want to try it. At least once."

"Really?"

"Yes. I trust you to make it good for me."

"You may not like it."

"Then, we never do it again."

"We never have to do it at all." His face was serious. "I'm not that into it."

"But you do like it, right?"

"Yeah, but I like putting my penis in your other holes better." His finger caressed her lower lip and slipped inside.

She sucked and his eyes darkened as she teased his finger with her tongue before pulling away. "If you don't want anal—"

"I never said I didn't want it."

She grinned. "Okay. Let me rephrase. If anal wasn't going to be what you picked when you won, what do you want?" Her body almost vibrated in anticipation. Sex with Nick was always wonderful and creative. Besides anal, she couldn't imagine what he'd ask her to do that they hadn't already done.

"Nothing." He glanced away. "There's nothing that we don't already do sexually that I want." He kissed her, whispering against her lips, "You are my wet dream come true."

She slid her tongue into his mouth, exploring. She wanted him again. He grabbed her ass, pulling her back onto his body. By the feel, he was more than ready for another round, but Nick always played to win. He was keeping something from her. She lifted off him, breaking the kiss. "You wanted something or you wouldn't have made me sign a paper."

"It's nothing." He shifted, pulling one of her legs over his hips and positioning her above his hard cock.

"It's not nothing." She scooted back on his legs. "Not when you won't tell me."

CHAPTER 29: NICK

"Fine." His temper snapped. Unbelievable. She was nothing but a mystery, an unopened book, and she was upset because *he* was keeping something from her. He rolled out from under her. "I was going to ask you to trust me enough to tell me the truth about why you're so fucking scared of marrying me and having kids." He stood, yanking the sheet off the bed and wrapping it around himself. So much for following the doc's orders and letting her take her time. "Yes, you had a miscarriage. It happens to women all the time but they go on and have healthy children."

"In my head, I know that"—she stared down at her hands—"but that doesn't matter because..." She wiped a tear from her cheek.

"Because why?" He sat on the bed. "Tell me. Please." He couldn't help her if she didn't tell him and her fear, her hurt killed him.

"Because...because I don't deserve kids." Tears streamed down her face. "I didn't want"—she hiccupped—

"the one I had. I don't deserve another."

"Oh Sarah, I'm a fucking idiot." He pulled her onto his lap. "I'm a guy. I didn't…I didn't understand." Who was he to think it was something to just get over, get past? He hadn't lost a child. He'd never carry one.

"It's okay." She rested her face against his chest.

"It isn't. I shouldn't push. I know better. I'm so fucking sorry." He kissed the side of her head.

She turned, her eyes wide and scared. "No. I'm sorry. There's more you should know."

This time Nick's heart stopped. What else had she gone through? What other nightmares had she not shared with him?

CHAPTER 30: SARAH

Sarah actually trembled on Nick's lap but she had to do this. He deserved to know the truth and he deserved her trust.

"Sarah...you don't have to..."

She touched his lips, silencing him. "I know. I want to." She smiled, wiping the tears from her checks. "That's a lie. Kind of. I don't but I do. Understand?"

He nodded.

"I...I am scared that I'll miscarry. That I don't deserve another child."

"You do deserve one. What happened was not your fault."

"Please." She touched his cheek. "I need to say this."

"Okay." He took her hand, intertwining their fingers.

"I'm also scared that...that this..." She kissed his hand. "Us. It's too good. It won't last. Something horrible is going to happen."

"Oh, babe." He pulled her close.

She rested her head on his shoulder. He understood. He knew her past. "I know it's not necessarily true but I can't shake the feeling and then you started talking about kids and all the fears got tangled up."

"I'll stop. I promise. I won't mention having kids again. You can let me know when you're ready."

"That's not fair to you. They'll be your kids too. You being ready is just as important as me being ready. I can't let you sacrifice what you want for me."

"But you want kids. So, I'm not sacrificing anything. I'm waiting."

"My sister miscarried three times. Once before Kyle and twice after. They stopped trying." She swallowed the big knot of fear. He deserved to know. She needed to let him decide, now before they married. "What if I can't carry to term?" Her voice came out whisper soft and she dropped her eyes to her lap. His breath froze. She could feel his dark gaze on her and she could tell the second he truly understood what she was asking. Truly understood her deepest fear.

He lifted her chin, forcing her to look at him. "Then we don't have kids or we adopt—"

"That's not fair to you." She tried to tamp down the hope in her eyes but she was pretty sure it shone like a light on a cloudy night.

"Fuck, Sarah. I'm not going to leave you if you can't have children." He kissed her forehead. "What do I have to do to convince you that I love you." He lifted their hands to his lips and kissed her knuckles. "I love *you*. I'll love you if

163

you can't get pregnant. I'll love you if you get pregnant every time I touch you."

"Every time?" She choked on her laugh. "Thank God, women can only get pregnant once every nine months or so because if I got knocked up every time you touched me, we'd have more than three kids a day."

"Bite your tongue." His lips caressed hers. "Or I'll do that for you."

She shivered, running her tongue along his lips but he pulled away.

"Seriously, Sarah. I love you. I'll love you forever."

"You can't know that." She shifted away from him. People always said that but they couldn't know. Life changed things.

"But I do." He captured her chin. "I'm old school and stubborn. When I say I'm going to do something, I do whatever it takes to accomplish it." He kissed her. "Will we have problems? Of course. Will we fight." His lips turned up in a sexy grin. "Absolutely, but makeup sex is great." His smile slid away. "Whatever life throws at us, we'll handle."

"And if we can't?" She wanted to believe him.

"We'll get help." His thumb skimmed over her cheek. "We'll talk. We'll remind each other and ourselves why we fell in love. We'll work at it. Sometimes it'll be hard but we'll get through it together. Okay?"

"Yeah." It sounded real. Not perfect, but real. "I'm sorry, I'm so difficult." She must be such a chore for him.

"Don't." His grip on her chin tightened. "Don't

apologize for being who you are."

"Even though, I'm fucked up?" Her words trembled in her throat.

"We're all fucked up in some way." He kissed her. "I love you. Everything about you." He grinned. "Even your fucked-up-edness."

"That's not a word." But it was the best sentence she'd ever heard.

"Doesn't matter." He kissed her forehead. "It's true."

She kissed him softly. "I'm trying to be more open with you. Let you in."

"I know."

"Thank you for being patient with me."

"I don't, of course, believe this, but I've heard that I'm not the easiest man to be around and that living with me is...difficult at best."

"Who told you that?" It was true, but she'd never said it out loud, not to her friends or even her sister.

"Ethan. Patrick. Terry. My brothers. My mom. Dad. Sisters. Do you want me to go on?"

"No. That's quite enough." She laughed and pushed on his chest. "What I want is for you to fuck me."

"That I can do but first." He rolled, pinning her under him. "I want to make sure we're good."

"We're good." She ran her leg up his, opening for him. "I'm a nut case and you're difficult to live with."

"That sums it up."

"But I'm getting better." She grinned. "What are you doing to be easier to live with?"

"My plan"—he shifted, running his cock along her seam, his hot tip pressing against her clit and making her moan—"is to keep you in a constant state of euphoria from orgasm that you don't notice my annoying habits."

"That's an excellent plan." She grabbed his dick, lining him up to her opening. "But you'd best get at it because I'm starting to get annoyed."

"No foreplay?"

"Next time." She put her feet on his ass and pulled. His nostrils flared as he slid inside her. "This time, just get to the fucking."

Thanks for reading *Playing House*.

I hope you enjoyed the story.

If you did, please leave a review. It's the greatest gift you can give an author.

See below for sneak peeks of Interviewing for her Lover (how Nick and Sarah met), The Voyeur (Patrick and Annie's story) and His Sub (Terry and Maggie's story). All three are free on all ebook retailers.

Join my newsletter and get the entire Six Nights of Sins series (Nick and Sarah's six nights of kinky fun) for free.

Ellis O. Day

Click the image above, go to my website,

www.EllisODay.com or email me for

details: authorellisoday@gmail.com

Interviewing For Her Lover

CHAPTER 1: SARAH

"Do I have to take off my clothes?" Sarah tugged on the hem of her black dress. It was shorter and lower cut in the front than she normally wore, but the Viewing was about finding a man for sex and according to Ethan men liked to look.

"No." Ethan turned her away from the door and forced her to look at him. "You don't have to do anything you don't want to do."

She stared into his blue eyes. Why couldn't he be interested in her? She'd only met with him five or six times, but she trusted him. He ran his business, La Petite Morte Club, very professionally and he was gorgeous with his sandy brown hair, strong cheekbones and vibrant blue eyes. Sex between them would be good. Easy. He was attractive and…not for her. She didn't want decent sex or good sex, she wanted mind blowing, screaming orgasms and that wouldn't happen between him and her because there was no chemistry, no attraction.

"Listen to me." He moved his hands to her shoulders and gave her a gentle shake. "You aren't selling yourself to the highest bidder. You're looking for a partner. One who'll"—he grinned—"turn you on in ways you can't even imagine."

She glanced at the door where the men waited. Waited for her. Waited to decide if they wanted to fuck her. "I'm a bit nervous."

"About what?"

This was embarrassing but she'd been honest with him up to this point. She'd had to be. He was helping her…had helped her to choose the five men in the other room. "What if none of them…"

"They will want you." He touched her chin, turning her face toward him. "A few of them may back out after this but not because they don't want you."

"Yeah, right."

"I'm only going to say this once. You're beautiful and

different, unique."

"That's not necessarily a good thing." She had long legs and a nice body—trim and firm—but with her auburn hair and green eyes she was cute at best, not gorgeous. The men she'd chosen were all rich, good looking and powerful. They could have anyone they wanted.

"It's exactly what they want, or most of them anyway." He took her hand and led her closer to the door.

She leaned on his arm, hating these shoes. She should've stuck with her flats but Ethan had given her a list of what she should wear and high heels were on the top. She'd found the smallest heels in the store and by Ethan's look when he'd first seen her she might've been better off going barefoot. He'd met her at the private entrance and his gaze had been appreciating as it'd skimmed over her dress, until he got to her feet. Then he'd frowned and shook his head.

"Finding the right men for you wasn't easy." He stopped at the door.

"Thanks a lot." She shifted away from him, his words hurting a little. She hadn't been sure of her appeal to the opposite sex in a long time, not since the early years with Adam.

"It's not because you aren't beautiful but because you want to be dominated and you want to dominate—"

"I do not want to dominate." All she could picture was a woman in black leather with a whip and that wasn't her, not at all.

"If you say so." He smiled a little. "But, you do want

to lead the scene. Right? Because that's what—"

"Yes." Her face was red. She could feel it. She didn't want to talk about her fantasies again. It'd been embarrassing enough the first time, but he'd had to know what she wanted to compile a list of candidates.

"Most at the club are either doms or subs. Very few are switches." His eyes raked over her. "That's what's so special about you. You want it all and…that's what made choosing these men difficult."

He'd given her a selection of twenty-two men who might be interested in what she wanted. She'd narrowed it down to seven. Two had been uninterested when he'd approached. That'd left her with the five who'd see her in person for the first time tonight, but she wouldn't see them. That'd come after the Viewing when she interviewed any who were still interested.

"Remember what you want. This is your deal. You call the shots. At least a little." He kissed her forehead. "But don't refuse to give them anything. You don't want a submissive."

"No." That didn't turn her on at all and she only had eight weeks. One night each week for two months before she'd go back to her lonely life, her lonely bed, dreaming of Adam.

"You can do this." He pulled a flask from his jacket and unscrewed the lid. "For courage."

"Thanks." She took a large swallow, the brandy too thick and sweet for her taste but it was better than nothing.

"Now, go find your lover."

She laughed a little but sadness swept through her. There'd be no love between this man and herself. This would be sex, fucking. That's all. The only man she'd ever love, her only lover, was dead. This was purely physical. "Thank you again." She stood on tip-toe and kissed his cheek. He may be gorgeous and run a sex club but he was a good man, a good friend.

She turned and opened the door and walked into the room, trying to stay balanced on these stupid heels. Men wouldn't find them so attractive if they had to wear them. The room was dark except for one light highlighting a small platform. That was for her. She stepped up onto the small stage. The room was silent but they were there, above her, hidden behind the one-way mirrors, watching and deciding if they wanted to take the next step—to eventually take her.

She stared into the blackness of the room. It wasn't huge but its emptiness made it seem vast. She glanced upward, the light making her squint and she quickly stared back into the darkness. This was arranged for them to see her. That was it. She'd get no glimpse of them yet. She'd seen their pictures, chosen them but meeting them in person would be different. A picture couldn't tell her their smell or the sound of their voices.

She tugged at her dress where it hugged her hips, wishing the questions would start, but there was only silence. She shifted, the heels already killing her feet. Ethan hadn't liked them and if they weren't going to impress, she might as well take them off. She moved to the back of the stage, leaned against the wall and removed her shoes. As she returned to the center of the stage a man spoke, his voice loud and commanding almost echoing throughout the room.

"Don't stop there. Take off your dress."

She bent, placing her shoes on the floor. That wasn't part of the deal. She wasn't going to undress in front of five men, only one. Only the one she chose. She straightened. "No."

"What?" He was surprised and not happy.

"I said no. That's not part of the Viewing."

"I want to see what I'm getting."

She stared up toward the windows, squinting a little. She couldn't tell from where the voice had come. The speaker system made it sound as if it were coming from God himself. "And you will if I pick you."

Another man laughed.

"It's not funny. She's disobedient," said the man with the loud voice.

"Not always. I can be obedient." These men liked to be in control but sometimes, so did she.

"Will you raise your dress? Just a little," asked another voice.

"Didn't you see enough in the photos?" She'd applied a few months ago for this one-time contract. She'd been excited and nervous when she'd received the acceptance email with an appointment for a photography session. She'd never had her picture professionally taken, since she didn't count school portraits or the ones her parents had had done at JCPenny's. She'd been anxious and a little turned on imaging wearing her new lingerie in front of a strange man, so she'd been disappointed to find the photographer was an elderly woman, but the lady had put her at ease and the photos had turned out better than she'd expected. She glanced up at the mirrors, hoping she wasn't disappointing all the men. That'd be too embarrassing.

"Those were…nice, but I'd like to see the real thing before deciding if you're worth my time."

She raised a brow. "You can always leave." She shouldn't antagonize him. She was sure the bossy man had already decided against committing to this agreement. Disobedience didn't appeal to him. That left four. If she didn't pick any of them, she could go through the process again, but she didn't think she would.

The man chuckled slightly. "I know that, but I haven't decided I don't want to fuck you. Not yet, anyway."

The word, so harsh and vulgar excited her. It was the truth. That was what she, what they were all deciding. Who'd get to fuck her. It was what she wanted, what she'd agreed to do, and as much as she dreaded it, she wanted it. She was tired of being alone. She missed having a man inside her—his tongue and fingers and cock.

"Do any of you have any questions?" She clasped her dress at her waist and slowly gathered it upward, displaying more and more of her long legs. She ran. They were in shape. The men would like them.

"Lower your top," said the same man who'd told her to take off her dress.

She didn't like him. If he didn't back out, she'd have Ethan remove him from her list. He was too commanding. He'd never allow her to be in control.

"I don't know if he's done looking at my legs yet." She continued raising the dress until her black and green lace panties were almost exposed.

"Very nice and thank you," said the polite man.

"You're welcome." This man might work. She shifted the dress up another inch before dropping it, giving them a glance at her panties.

"Now, your top," said the bossy guy.

She lowered her spaghetti string off one shoulder, letting the dress dip, but not enough to show anything besides the side of her bra.

"More," he said.

"No." She raised the strap, covering herself. She didn't like this man and wished he'd leave. She'd kick him out but that wasn't part of the process and they were very firm about their rules at this club.

"He got to see your pussy. Why don't I get to see your tits?"

"You got to see as much as he did." She was ready to move on. She bent and picked up her shoes. "If there's nothing else, gentleman, we can set up times for the interview process."

"Turn around," said another man.

It was a command, but she didn't mind. There was a politeness to his order and something about the texture of his voice caused an ache between her thighs. There was a caress in his tone but with an edge and a promise of a good hard fuck.

"Are you going to obey?" His words were whisper soft and smooth.

"Yes." That was going to be part of this too. Her commanding and him commanding. She dropped her shoes and turned.

"Raise you dress again."

She looked over her shoulder at where she imagined he sat watching her.

"Please." There was humor in his tone.

She smiled and slowly gathered the dress upward. She stopped right below the curve of her bottom.

"More. Please." There was a little less humor in his voice.

She wanted to show him her ass. She wanted to show that voice everything but not with the others around. This would be just her and one man, one stranger. That was one of her rules. "No. Only if you're picked do you get to see any more of me than you have." She dropped her dress, grabbed her shoes and walked off the stage and out the door.

She was going to have sex with a stranger. She was going to live out her fantasies for eight nights with a man she didn't know and would never really know, but she wasn't going to lose who she was. She'd keep her honor and her dignity which meant she had to pick a man who'd agree with her rules.

Get your free copy and find out what happens next.

https://books2read.com/u/3nYKo6

The Voyeur

CHAPTER 1: ANNIE

Annie finished making the bed and gathered the sheets from the floor, keeping them as far away from her body as possible. These sex rooms were disgusting and Ethan was a jerk making her work as a maid. She almost had her Bachelor's Degree in Culinary Arts, but he'd refused to hire her for the kitchen—too many men in the kitchen. The only job he'd give her at La Petite Mort Club was as a maid and unfortunately, she needed the money too badly to refuse.

She stuffed the dirty sheets into the cart and hurried out the door. She had almost thirty minutes before she had to be at the next "sex room." She hid the cart in a closet and darted down a back hallway, staying clear of the cameras. Julie, the woman who supervised the daytime maids, was a real bitch. If she were caught sneaking away from her duties, she'd be assigned to the orgy rooms every day. Right now, they all took turns cleaning that nightmare. She swore they should get hazard pay to even go in those rooms.

She slipped through a doorway and hurried to the one-way mirror. She stared at the couple in the next room. From her first day here, she'd been curious about the activities at the club. She was twenty-four and wasn't a virgin but she'd never, ever done some of these things.

The woman in the room below was tied to a table, legs spread and wearing some sort of leather outfit that left her large breasts free and her crotch exposed. She had shaved her pussy and her pink lower lips were swollen and glistening from her excitement. The man strolled around the table as if he had all night. He still had his pants on but had removed his shirt. His arms and chest were well defined but he had a slight paunch. His erection tented his pants and Annie felt wetness pool between her legs. She had no idea why watching this turned her on but it did.

Ever since she'd accidentally barged in on that guy and girl in the Interview room, she couldn't stop watching.

The man below ran his hand up the woman's inner thigh, glancing over her pussy. The woman thrust her hips upward and Annie ran her own hand between her legs. The man's mouth moved but Annie couldn't hear anything and then he slapped the woman across the thigh hard enough to leave a red mark. Annie jumped. She wasn't into that, but she couldn't stop watching the woman's face. At first, it'd contorted in pain but then it'd morphed into pleasure. The man hit her again and then bent, kissing the red welts— running his tongue across them as his fingers squeezed her nipple.

Annie clutched her thighs together, searching for some relief. Her panties were soaked. It wouldn't take but a few strokes to make her come. She started to slide her hand into her pants.

"Having fun?" asked a deep voice from behind her.

She spun around, her heart dropping into her stomach. "Ah...I was just finishing cleaning in here." Damn, she should've closed the door but she hadn't expected anyone in this area. The rooms were off limits on this floor until tonight and she was the only one assigned to clean here.

He shut the door and locked it before strolling toward her. She'd seen him around the Club, but more than that she remembered him from the military photos her brother, Vic, had sent to her. She carried one of the three of them—Vic, Ethan and this guy, Patrick—in her purse. He'd been attractive in the picture, but now that he was older and in person he was gorgeous. He had dark green eyes, brown hair and a perfect body. He stopped so close to her his chest almost brushed against her breasts. She was pretty sure it would if she inhaled deeply. She really wanted to take that deep breath and feel his hard chest against her breasts.

"Don't let me stop you from enjoying the show."

"I…I wasn't. I should go." She started to walk past him but he grabbed her hand.

His grip was warm and strong but loose enough that she could pull free if she wanted. She didn't. Even though she only knew him from her brother's pictures and letters, she'd had many fantasies about him when she'd been in high school. Her gaze dropped to the front of his pants and her mouth almost watered. He was definitely interested. She dragged her eyes up his body, stopping on his face. He smiled at her.

"There's nothing to be embarrassed about. Watching turns us all on." He kissed the back of her hand and she jumped as his tongue darted out, tasting her skin.

"I…I should go." She didn't move.

"No, you should watch." He dropped her hand and grabbed her shoulders, gently turning her toward the mirror. He trailed his hands up and down her arms. "Watch."

The man in the other room was now sucking on the woman's breast as his fingers caressed her pussy.

"Would you like to hear them? Or do you like it quiet?" His voice was a rough whisper against her ear.

"Sound, please." She wanted to hear their gasps and moans. She wanted to close her eyes and pretend it was her. She shifted, squeezing her thighs together.

He chuckled as he moved away. She felt his absence to her bones. He'd been strong and warm behind her and for a moment she'd felt safe, safer than she had since her brother had come back from the war, broken and sad, and her father had started drinking again.

The woman's moans filled the room and Patrick came back to stand behind her, this time placing his hands on her waist.

"I'm Patrick," he said against her ear.

She couldn't take her eyes from the scene in front of her. The woman was almost coming as the man thrust his fingers inside of her.

"What's your name?" He nipped her neck and she jumped.

"I…I…" If she told him her name, he might say something to Ethan. Ethan would kill her if he knew she was in here watching.

"Tell me your name." His lips trailed along her neck and she tipped her head giving him better access.

The guy was kissing his way down the woman's body. Annie wanted to touch herself, to make herself come but Patrick was here.

He nibbled her ear. "Why won't you tell me your name?"

"I…I'll get in trouble." She rubbed her ass against his erection, hopefully giving him a hint.

"Tease." His hand drifted down her stomach, stopping right above where she wanted him to touch. "Tell me your name or I'll make you suffer." He unbuttoned her pants and left his hand—warm, rough but immobile—resting on her abdomen.

"I can't." She stood on tip-toe, hoping his hand would lower a little but he was too tall or she was too short. He had to be almost six foot and she was barely five-foot four. "I could get fired and I need this job."

"Darling, Ethan won't fire you for fucking a customer."

"We can't." She spun around. She hadn't thought this through. He was her fantasy come to life and she wanted him to be hers just for a moment, but Ethan would find out and then she'd be in deep shit.

"Don't worry. I'm a member and you work here, so we're both clean." He hesitated, his hands tightening on her hips. "Are you protected?"

"What?" She had no idea what he was talking about.

"Ethan makes sure everyone at the Club is clean but only the…some of his employees are required to be on birth control." He ran his hands up her sides, getting closer and closer to her breasts. "Are you on birth control?" His eyes darkened as they dropped to her tits. "If not, it's okay. There are other things we can do."

Oh, she wanted to do everything his eyes promised, but she couldn't. "No, I'll get in trouble. I need this job. I have to go." She tried to move but her feet refused to obey, so she just stared at his handsome face.

"Are you sure?" He bent so he was almost eye level with her. "I promise. Ethan won't care. A lot of maids become…change jobs. The pay's a lot better." His eyes roamed over her frame. "Especially, for someone as cute as you."

Ethan would kill her before letting her become one of his pleasure associates.

"I could talk to Ethan for you." His hands moved up her body, stopping right below her breasts.

Her nipples hardened and she forgot everything but what he was making her feel. He ran his thumb over one of them and she leaned closer, wanting him to do it again.

He did. He continued rubbing her nipple as he spoke. "I could persuade him to let me…handle your initiation into club life."

Her heart raced in her chest. It could be just her and him doing all these things she'd seen. Her pussy throbbed but she couldn't do it. She wouldn't do it. She couldn't have sex for money. Her parents were both dead but they'd never understand and she couldn't disappoint them. "No. I can't do that…not for money." Her eyes darted to the door. She needed to get out of there before she did something she'd regret.

"That's even better." He smiled as he stepped closer. "We can keep this between us. No money. Only a man and a woman." He leaned down and whispered in her ear, "Giving each other pleasure. A lot of pleasure. In ways you haven't even imagined."

There were moans from the other room and she glanced over her shoulder. The man's face was buried between the woman's thighs.

Patrick turned her around, pulling her against him and wrapping his arms around her waist. "Are you wet?"

"What? No." She struggled in his arms, her ass brushing against his erection again.

"Oh fuck. Do that again." He kissed her neck, open mouthed and hot.

She stopped trying to get away. She wanted this…this moment. She shouldn't but she did, so she wiggled her butt against him again. He was hard and long and her body ached for him. It'd been too long she'd had sex. She needed this.

"Would you like me to touch you?" His hands drifted over her hips and down her thighs.

She'd like him to do all sorts of things to her. She nodded.

"Say it." His words were a command she couldn't disobey.

"Yes."

"Yes, what?" He untucked her shirt from her pants.

"Touch me. Please." She was already pushing her hips toward his hand. She wanted his hand on her, his fingers inside of her.

"Are you wet?" he asked again.

She inhaled sharply as he unzipped her pants.

"Don't lie to me. I'll find out in a minute."

She'd never talked dirty during sex and she wasn't sure she was ready to do that with a stranger. Her heart skipped a beat. Maybe she shouldn't be doing any of this with a stranger. She grabbed his hand. "Maybe we shouldn't."

The woman below cried out and the man straightened, wiping his face and unbuttoning his pants.

"Watch. The main event is about to happen." Patrick's hot breath tickled her neck.

Her gaze locked on the man's penis. It was large and demanding. He straddled the woman, grabbing his cock.

"Don't you want to feel some of what they feel?" He nibbled on her ear and then neck. "I can help you."

She may not know him, but she trusted him. He was a former marine. He'd been a good friend of Vic's. He wouldn't hurt her and she needed to come. She loosened her grip, letting go of his hand. He slipped inside her pants, caressing her pussy through her underwear. His fingers were long and strong. She closed her eyes, leaning against him as he stroked her.

"You're already so wet and hot." His breath was a warm caress on her ear. "But, I'm going to make you wetter and then, I'm going to make you come." His other hand shoved her pants down, giving him more room to work. "Open your eyes and watch the show."

She did as he said. The man was inside the woman, thrusting hard and fast. The woman was moaning and trying to move but the restraints kept her mostly helpless.

"Fuck, you're soaked." Patrick's hand cupped her and she arched into his touch, rubbing her ass against his erection. He shoved his hand inside her underwear, his finger running along her folds until he slipped one inside.

"Oh." She grabbed his hand—not to push him away, but to make sure he didn't leave.

He smiled against her hair. "Don't worry, baby. I won't stop." He stroked his finger inside of her and his wrist brushed against her clit.

She needed more. She needed to touch him, feel him. She turned her head, wrapping her arms up and around his neck. He kissed her. It was desperate and wild, but he stopped too soon.

"They're almost done. You don't want to miss it."

She turned back to the mirror. The man below continued to fuck the woman as Patrick finger-fucked her. His other hand slipped under her shirt to her breast. His lips sucked her neck as he rocked his erection against her ass. He was everywhere, and she was so close. The muscles in her legs constricted. Her hips tipped upward.

"Wait, baby," he groaned in her ear, as he pushed a second finger inside of her. "Just a few more minutes."

His fingers were stretching her and it felt wonderful. She moaned, long and low as he thrust harder and faster, almost matching the pace of the man in the other room. She could almost imagine it was Patrick's cock and not his fingers inside of her.

"Oh...oh," she cried out. He was pushing her toward the edge. Her body was spiraling with each pump of his fingers. She was going to come—right here while watching that couple. It was so dirty and so wrong and it only made her hotter.

The woman below screamed and her body stiffened. The man thrust again and again and then grunted his release.

"Show's over." Patrick nipped her neck at the same time he pressed down on her clit with his thumb, sending her shooting into her orgasm.

She trembled and he pulled her close, his hand still cupping her pussy and his fingers still inside of her. When her heartbeat had settled, he removed his hand and bent, pulling off her shoes and removing her pants before lifting her and carrying her to the wall.

"My turn." He wrapped her legs around his waist.

Her phone rang. "My work phone. I...I have to answer it."

"When we're done." He unzipped his pants.

"Annie, answer the phone. I know you're around here. I can hear it ringing you stupid bitch," yelled Julie.

"Oh, shit." She shoved Patrick away, and ran across the room, grabbing her clothes off the floor. "It's my boss. She'll kill me if she finds me like this."

"I'll take care of Julie." He headed for the door, zipping up his fly. "Don't move." He grinned over his shoulder at her. "You can take off your pants again, but other than that, don't move."

"No. Please." She raced over to him, grabbing his arm. "I need this job." And Ethan could not find out about this.

"She won't fire you. She can't. Only Ethan can fire you." He bent and kissed her.

His lips were gentle and coaxing this time and her body swayed into him. He pulled her even closer and she could feel his cock, thick and heavy, pushing against her. Her pussy tightened again in anticipation.

"Damnit, Annie. This is going to be so much worse if I have to call your stupid phone again. Get out here!" Julie was only a few doors down.

She grabbed Patrick and tugged on his hand. "Please, hide." She glanced around, looking for somewhere that would conceal a six-foot muscular man.

"I'm not going to hide from Julie."

Get your free copy and find out what happens next.

HTTPS://BOOKS2READ.COM/U/BXQBMK

The His Sub

CHAPTER 1: TERRY

Terry wandered through the crowd of well-dressed women and men at La Petite Mort Club. It was the same scene every time Ethan, his friend and owner of the Club, threw one of these events. The members mingled with the newbies, hoping to snag something different or someone interesting.

Ethan strolled casually toward him, a ready smile on

his face as he greeted his guests. "Terry, about time you made it down here."

"Like you can talk." His friend spent most of his time in the back office, watching the Club on monitors.

"I've been mingling for over an hour."

"It's your business not mine." He leaned against the balustrade, peering down on the crowd.

"True, but you could sell your practice and buy me out."

"And run this place?" He laughed. "No thank you." He tossed back his scotch. "I spend enough time here as it is." He used to practically live here except when he was at the office or in court, but lately he'd been staying home more.

"Good turn out tonight." Ethan waved at a waitress and a moment later they each had another drink.

"Yeah, but I don't see one interesting person in this crop of wannabe members."

"And you can tell if someone is interesting just by looking at them?"

"I can tell not one of them has an original thought. Look at them. They're all in red." The Club was awash in a sea of red dresses—short, long, dark, light but always red.

"It is a Valentine's Day party."

"I know but you'd think one woman"—he held up his finger—"one would consider that everyone else would be in red and wear a different color."

"There are some pinks out there."

"Same thing, just lighter."

Ethan grabbed his phone from his pocket and looked at

the text, frowning.

"Problem?" The Club was usually a safe place but on open night events, when Ethan allowed non-members access in order to recruit new members, the place could get dangerous.

"A little skirmish over a woman." Ethan grinned, his blue eyes sparkling as a couple of young guys hurried past them, almost tripping in their haste to stay close to a group of very attractive women. "These youngsters haven't learned that sharing is more fun."

He ignored Ethan's teasing. He'd taken a lot of shit from Ethan, Nick and even Patrick because he wasn't into the sharing thing. He preferred it to be him and one woman, one sweet, little sub. Since he was in no mood to listen to any more crap, he'd change the subject. "Those kids barely look old enough to drink."

"You're showing your age." Ethan patted his shoulder. "You should find some nice, young thing and teach her how to please her master."

"Maybe I will, if any of them show enough originality to dress in something other than red."

"I've got to go and sort out this problem." Ethan slid his phone into his pocket. "I'll find you later. If you find that elusive non-red dress, I'd suggest we share but..." He chuckled as he headed down the stairs, maneuvering through the crowd like he had nowhere to go, when in reality he was heading for the back—the playrooms.

Terry's eyes stopped and lingered on the new hire, Desiree, who was moving around the room, talking and flirting with all the men and some women. She was interesting—exotic and smart—but there was a shrewdness behind her eyes that he'd learned a long time ago to avoid. A woman like her had an agenda and she stuck with it, no matter what.

Someone slammed into his back, causing his drink to spill down his front, staining his shirt and suit.

"Oh…oh, I'm so sorry."

He spun around and encountered a red dress and breasts—milky white and lush. The skin would be fragrant and softer than rose petals.

"Oh. Your shirt. Let me get something to wipe that up."

He forced his eyes away from those lovely breasts. Her hair was a rich mahogany. It'd probably hang past her shoulders in waves of curly silk but right now it was piled haphazardly on her head in what had been some kind of elegant style before disobedient strands had escaped their restraint. She looked mussed and damnit, he wanted to be the one to muss her.

"Paper towels? Napkins?" She glanced around and then hurried over to the bar.

She was short and curvy—her body succulent, ripe and he'd bet juicy. She grabbed a stack of napkins and headed for him. Her dress was too tight, like she'd recently gained some weight. He usually went for the tall, athletic types but for some reason his dick had picked this woman.

She returned to his side and dabbed at the wetness on his shirt and jacket as if she actually gave a shit about his clothes. This was no subtle caress, no flirtation—just indifferent efficiency.

"I'm so sorry." She wadded the napkins in her hand, still patting at his clothes.

"You said that already." His words came out gruffer than he'd meant. No one treated him with disinterest. He was a rich, successful, attractive man and she was treating him like a child. He wanted to pull up her—unfortunately, red—dress and fuck her right here. They were at the Club. It wasn't out of the question.

Her hand froze. "Oh." Her large hazel eyes looked startled and then hurt. "Sorry. Ah, excuse me." She headed toward the stairs, dropping the wet napkins in the trash before disappearing in the crowd.

He turned around, so he could see the first floor and waited for her to appear. She hurried across the downstairs room, bumping and stumbling through the crowd. A lone, scared, little rabbit in a room full of predators. She stopped for a moment, scanning the crowd as if searching for someone.

"Who are you looking for, little rabbit?" he mumbled to himself. "A husband? Boyfriend?" He grinned as he lifted his scotch to his lips. "Girlfriend?" He frowned at the empty glass. "You spilled my drink. I'll forgive you, but it's going to cost you." He waved at one of the waitresses. "Everything has a price, little rabbit." As one of the best divorce lawyers in town, he knew that better than anyone.

The waitress brought him another drink. He paid, giving her a large tip before turning to find his little rabbit.

He took a sip of the scotch, enjoying the smooth burn and his lush little bunny's journey through La Petite Mort Club. She froze in her tracks, her jaw dropping open as she gazed at a threesome on one of the couches.

The woman was sandwiched between two men, stroking one's cock as the other man fondled her beneath her red dress. The man behind her looked up and said something to the little rabbit. Her face heated and Terry's eyes dropped to her chest. Yep, they were a pretty shade of pink but what he really wanted to know was if the color matched her pussy.

She stumbled away from the threesome, bumping into another man. It was Richard, who stopped her from falling and then immediately let her go, stepping away. She was safe with Richard. As a member of the Club and a gentleman, he knew that safewords were law and consent was absolutely necessary. She said something to Richard and continued through the Club, disappearing in the crowd.

"You're not getting away that easily." He followed along on the upper floor, keeping her in sight. He had no idea why but he wanted her. Maybe it was simply because she was different than everyone else here.

He took another sip of his drink. It was obviously the little rabbit's first time at a place like this but she didn't seem eager to participate or interested in watching. She truly seemed to be looking for someone specific—not just someone to fuck. Well, she'd found the latter because he was going to fuck her. In the office he followed his head but at La Petite Mort Club his cock was king.

She headed toward the playrooms. There was no way he was going to miss this. He sauntered down the stairs, grabbing another drink on the way. She wasn't hard to follow. She left a path of irritated people in her wake as she bumped into them and apologized profusely before hurrying forward. Her full, round hips swayed under her tight, red dress that'd seen better days—hem frayed and at least five years out of style. Not that he minded, especially the snug fit of the cloth, but his women were usually much more put tougher.

They were the CEO types—women who thrived on being in charge. He enjoyed teaching them how much fun turning over control could be. When they were with him, he was their dom, their master and he made sure they loved every second. He told them when to kneel, when to suck, when to spread their legs or ass and when to come. The more power they had in their everyday life the more they craved bowing to his wishes. His little rabbit wouldn't know what power was. She was a hot mess of a woman. Still, his dick wanted her, so his dick would have her.

She was hurrying out of the first playroom when he entered the hallway. Her eyes were huge and her cheeks were on fire. She ducked into the next room and quickly came out—even redder than before.

"Excuse me." He'd offer his assistance in her search. She'd be grateful. He could capitalize on that unless she was looking for her husband or boyfriend. He wasn't in the mood to share. He would, however, allow the other man to watch. He could give the guy some pointers on how to take care of his wife because this woman obviously needed guidance.

"You?" Her eyes narrowed.

That wasn't the reaction he was used to. Women usually purred for him.

"Are you following me?"

"What would you do if I said I was?" He took a step toward her.

"I'd scream. There are bouncers here. I saw them."

Lord, she was cute. "Yes, but if they came running at every little scream they'd die of exhaustion."

As if to emphasis his point a woman screamed in ecstasy. His little rabbit's face heated and she averted her gaze.

"Who are you looking for?" He ran his finger lightly down her cheek. Her skin was as smooth as porcelain but much warmer and softer.

"Ah..." Her breath hitched, making her breasts swell dangerously above her gown.

He could have her out of it in a minute. The skin would be even softer than that on her face. "Did you lose your husband?"

"No." She licked her lips.

There was no way he could let that offer pass. He slowly bent, giving her time to refuse him. He may command his women but he made sure they always wanted it first. Her eyes dropped to his mouth and he couldn't help a slight smirk. She wanted this as much as he did. He moved closer and let his lips rest gently on hers. He'd take it slow, make her yearn for him and then he'd make her obey.

"What are you doing?" She turned her head.

"Kissing you." His lips brushed against her cheek. He wasn't about to lose ground.

"Why?" She turned again, her eyes meeting his.

The confusion in her hazel gaze was as obvious as the hideous dress on her gorgeous body. She may remind him of a rabbit but she couldn't be that naive. She had to be in her mid to late thirties.

He should use flowery words—tell her she was beautiful, desirable—but that wasn't him. Blunt was the kindest word to describe him. "Because, I want to."

"You don't even know me."

He was losing ground. The interest in her face was being replaced with disgust. "No, but I know I want you." Damn, he shouldn't have said that.

"Well, too bad." She pushed on his chest and he stepped back, letting her pass.

"This is a sex club, you know." He followed. "If you aren't here for sex, why are you here?"

She spun around. "I'm quite aware of what this place is and just because I don't want you, a stranger to…to"—she waved her hand about—"in the hallway."

He laughed. "We wouldn't be the first. There are people fucking in the main room."

"I know. I saw." Her cheeks heated.

He stepped closer. "You are adorable." He touched a strand of hair that was resting on her shoulder. It was like satin.

"I'm a mess." She pulled her hair free from his fingers.

"A hot mess. A fiery, hot, sexy mess." He moved closer with every other word. "One I want to fuck, right now."

Her eyes hardened. "Too bad because I don't"—again she waved her hand about—"you know, with strangers in the hallway." She shoved his chest again.

He took a small step back but he wasn't giving up yet. "We can go to a private room."

"No."

Shit. By the look on her face, he'd just made a bigger blunder.

"Let me go." She pushed him again.

Damn. She'd said the worst three words in the English language besides I love you. He moved away, releasing her for the moment. "Sorry."

She harrumphed.

"I made a mistake."

"Yes, you did." She hurried down the hallway but not before he'd seen the look of hurt in her large eyes.

"What the fuck do you want from me? I made a mistake and apologized." He trailed after her.

"I want you to leave me alone. Please. Go away."

He stopped. His little rabbit was running but perhaps, he shouldn't chase. She darted down a hallway toward the hardcore BDSM rooms.

Normally, she'd be fine—embarrassed but fine. Except with all the newbies here, tonight wasn't a normal night. He hurried after her. "Hey, I don't think you want to go—"

"Leave me alone." She walked faster. "I need to find my friend and get out of here."

"Okay, but I don't—"

"Go away." She sounded both mad and as if she were going to cry.

"Suit yourself, but I warned you."

She strode into the closest room. He should leave. Let her find out that he wasn't the worst thing in a place like this, not in a long shot, but his feet followed her. She was his little rabbit. He'd found her. No one else was going to enjoy her until he'd had his taste.

"Vicky? Vicky? Are you in here?"

He stepped into the room, staying in the shadows. She was looking around in the dark for her friend. It only took a moment for one of the six guys to notice the little rabbit who'd stumbled into their den.

"Shit," he mumbled. Not one of those guys was a regular.

Grab your free copy and find out what happens next.
https://www.EllisODay.com
https://books2read.com/u/3yrBlV

BOOKS BY ELLIS O. DAY

LA PETITE MORT CLUB SERIES

SIX NIGHTS OF SIN SERIES
Six Nights of Sin -The Complete Series: Books 1-6
HTTPS://BOOKS2READ.COM/U/3NEDAR

Interviewing For Her Lover (Book 1) **(Free)**
HTTPS://BOOKS2READ.COM/U/3NYKO6
Taking Control (Book 2)
HTTPS://BOOKS2READ.COM/U/MDKBKR
School Fantasy (Book 3)
HTTPS://BOOKS2READ.COM/U/BP1PER
Master-Slave Fantasy (Book 4)
HTTPS://BOOKS2READ.COM/U/BQZ8JD
Punishment Fantasy (Book 5)
HTTPS://BOOKS2READ.COM/U/MZW9EE
The Proposition (Book 6)
HTTPS://BOOKS2READ.COM/U/3KZR5L

THE VOYEUR SERIES
THE VOYEUR **(FREE)**
HTTPS://BOOKS2READ.COM/U/BXQBMK
Watching The Voyeur (Book 2)
HTTPS://BOOKS2READ.COM/U/3J0E2J
Touching The Voyeur (Book 3)
HTTPS://BOOKS2READ.COM/U/MGRR66

Loving The Voyeur (Book 4)
HTTPS://BOOKS2READ.COM/U/4AW2PQ

The Voyeur Series (Books 1-4)
HTTPS://BOOKS2READ.COM/U/BZAB9Z

SIX WEEKS OF SEDUCTION
HTTPS://BOOKS2READ.COM/U/3R11YG

A MERRY MASQUERADE FOR CHRISTMAS
HTTPS://BOOKS2READ.COM/U/38R7EV

THE DOM'S SUBMISSION SERIES
The Dom's Submission Box Set (Books 1-3)
HTTPS://BOOKS2READ.COM/U/BA27KQ

His Sub (Book 1) (**Free Ebook**)
HTTPS://BOOKS2READ.COM/U/3YRBLV

His Mission (Book 2)
HTTPS://BOOKS2READ.COM/U/4AQEOO

His Submission (Book 3)
HTTPS://BOOKS2READ.COM/U/49OZED

LA PETITE MORT CLUB INTIMATE ENCOUNTERS SERIES
(You know the players but do you know the kink?)

His Lesson (More Terry And Maggie)
HTTPS://BOOKS2READ.COM/U/4XZPN9

COMING SOON:

Terry and Maggie's second night at the Club

Ethan's Story

Mattie's Story

Vic's Story

Rebecca's Story

Email me with questions, concerns or to let
me know what you thought of the book. I
love hearing from readers.
authorellisoday@gmail.com

Follow me
www.EllisODay.com

Facebook

https://www.facebook.com/EllisODayRomanceAuthor/

Twitter

https://twitter.com/ellis_o_day

Pinterest

http://www.pinterest.com/AuthorEllisODay

ABOUT THE AUTHOR

Ellis O. Day loves reading and writing about love and sex. She believes that although the two don't have to go together, it's best when they do (both in life and in fantasy).